Christmas at the Harrington Park Hotel

From London, with love...

It's official! The Harrington Park Hotel is finally
back in the hands of the family that founded it. And
James, Sally and Hugo—the children of the hotel's
late and great owner, Rupert—are determined
to return it to its former glory. Just in time for the
festive season!

But it's not just the Harrington Park Hotel that could
do with a little holiday magic... It's the love lives of
the Harrington siblings, who until now had drifted
apart. This Christmas in Regent's Park, redemption
and love might be closer than they think.

Discover Chloe and James's story in
Christmas Reunion in Paris by Liz Fielding
Available now!

Read Edward and Sally's story in
Their Royal Baby Gift by Kandy Shepherd

And look out for Erin and Hugo's story in
Stolen Kiss with Her Billionaire Boss by Susan Meier
Coming soon!

Dear Reader,

Writing is hard work. Honestly. You'd think that working from home, never having to get out of your jammies—although it tends to startle the mailman—with the kettle within reach and endless quantities of your favourite biscuit on hand (Fox's Jam 'n' Cream Rings if you're interested) would be a piece of cake. Or maybe a biscuit.

This is not so.

The back complains, the brain does not always cooperate, the eyes get gritty. I know, first world problems.

But then, once in a while, a book comes along that gives you the excuse to do something wild, behave the way the world believes romantic novelists live. Like hopping on the Eurostar and spending a weekend in Paris because that is where your book is set. And going to Galeries Lafayette with its amazing Christmas tree and riding around the city in an open-top bus—a bit cold in the last weekend in November, but no rain or snow. And call it *work*!

I had fun and I hope you do, too, when you join Chloe and James as they meet again in *Christmas Reunion in Paris*.

With love,

Liz

Christmas Reunion in Paris

Liz Fielding

Special thanks and acknowledgment are given to
Liz Fielding for her contribution to the
Christmas in the Harrington Park Hotel miniseries.

Recycling programs
for this product may
not exist in your area.

ISBN-13: 978-1-335-55646-2

Christmas Reunion in Paris

Copyright © 2020 by Harlequin Books S.A.

For questions and comments about the quality of this book,
please contact us at CustomerService@Harlequin.com.

Harlequin Enterprises ULC
22 Adelaide St. West, 40th Floor
Toronto, Ontario M5H 4E3, Canada
www.Harlequin.com

Printed in U.S.A.

Liz Fielding was born with itchy feet. She made it to Zambia before her twenty-first birthday and, gathering her own special hero and a couple of children on the way, lived in Botswana, Kenya and Bahrain—with pauses for sightseeing pretty much everywhere in between. She now lives in the west of England, close to the Regency grandeur of Bath and the ancient mystery of Stonehenge, and these days lets her pen do the traveling.

For news of upcoming books visit Liz's website, lizfielding.com.

Books by Liz Fielding

Harlequin Romance

Destination Brides

A Secret, a Safari, a Second Chance

Summer at Villa Rosa

Her Pregnancy Bombshell

Romantic Getaways

The Sheikh's Convenient Princess

Tempted by Trouble
Flirting with Italian
The Last Woman He'd Ever Date
Vettori's Damsel in Distress
The Billionaire's Convenient Bride

Harlequin KISS

Anything but Vanilla...
For His Eyes Only

Visit the Author Profile page at Harlequin.com for more titles.

Writing a miniseries with authors you love is a joy.

Thank you Kandy Shepherd and Susan Meier for sharing the Christmas at the Harrington Park Hotel experience with me.

And thank you to my editor, Bryony Green, who never once nagged, but waited patiently for me to get my act together and deliver the book!

Praise for
Liz Fielding

CHAPTER ONE

*City Diary, London Evening Post,
28th September*

*Following a meeting with creditors of the
Harrington Park Hotel, the owner, Nicholas Wolfe, announced today that he has filed
for bankruptcy.*

*Once a name breathed with a sigh of pleasure, the hotel was considered a home away
from home by those wealthy enough to enjoy
the Harrington experience. But the hotel
began to lose its way following the death of
Rupert Harrington two decades ago.*

*Katherine, his widow, handed ownership
of the hotel to her second husband, American
businessman Nicholas Wolfe, in order to concentrate on her young family. Wolfe lacked the
magic Harrington touch, however, and under
his stewardship the brand lost its sparkle. Following Katherine's death in a road accident
the hotel's decline, while slow, was terminal.*

Rumour has it that James Harrington,

owner of the Michelin-starred restaurant L'Étranger, and the younger son of Katherine and Rupert Harrington, has teamed up with his interior designer twin, Sally Harrington, to put together a bid, hoping to restore this iconic London hotel to its former glory.

CHLOE WAS RUNNING LATE. She should be on her way to another job, but an outbreak of flu had left the hotel short-handed and when the head of Housekeeping had asked her to extend her shift, refusal had not been an option.

The double shift had left her exhausted, her legs, feet, head were aching, but this was the last guestroom. The room had been booked for a late arrival, but she was running out of time.

Always uneasy about being upstairs when guests were beginning to return from shopping or sightseeing, she worked fast, but it had to be perfect. She needed this job and mentally ticked off a checklist, ensuring that everything was exactly as a guest who was staying in a luxurious boutique hotel in the heart of Paris would expect.

The small fridge was fully stocked. The flowers perfect, the fruit without a blemish. A bottle of mineral water stood beside a gleaming glass. A small pink-lidded box containing two light-as-air *macarons* was on the tray beside the coffee machine.

She took a breath, momentarily swept back to the taste of raspberry and rose petals melting in her mouth. A long-ago treat from the boy she loved…

She'd spent too long daydreaming and the click of the key in the lock brought her back to reality with the arrival of *madame* to check the room.

'*J'ai terminé…*'

'*Prends ton temps, madame…*' The man's tone was reassuring, not *madame*, but the guest telling her to take her time as he dropped his bag and crossed to the window.

He spoke in French and his accent was good, but he was English and her hand trembled as she smoothed back the cover.

A complaint would have been bad, but far worse was the risk that she would come face to face with someone who might recognise her. Someone who had attended the same exclusive private boarding school.

News of where she was, what she was doing—in mocking tones of scandalised amusement—would be flashed around social media within hours. She would have to leave Paris, start again somewhere else. That would cost money, put her dream further out of reach.

The possibility, she told herself, was vanishingly small. She took a breath, reminded herself that staff were invisible. Even if she did come face to face with someone with whom she'd been at school, someone who knew her parents, they would only see the white shirt, the black waistcoat and skirt.

The uniform, not the person.

She straightened from her task, took one last glance around. The man was staring out at Paris, already ablaze with lights for the Christmas season, but she didn't see the view, only the face mirrored in the glass.

Chloe gasped his name.

'James…'

It was no more than a whispered breath, but his gaze flickered from the lights of the city to her own image mirrored alongside him.

For a moment, as they looked into the reflection of each other's eyes, her heart stood still. Would he recognise her? Remember her?

The thought had barely formed before he spun around so fast that, as if he had disturbed the earth's rotation, the room rocked.

She flung out a hand as her world tilted, throwing her off balance, but there was only air to grasp until strong fingers clasped hers, his body steadying her world as he stepped into her, supporting her, holding her, saying her name.

Not a ghost, but the living man with whom,

a lifetime ago, she had shared an intense, passionate teenage love.

A doomed romance that had brought disaster down on both their heads but, in his arms, she had forgotten reality, naively blanked from her mind the future planned for her by ambitious parents.

For a few short months, lying spooned against his body, feeling the slow, steady thud of his heart beating against her ribs, the softness of his sleeping breath against her neck, anything had seemed possible.

Now, unbelievably, he was here, grown into the promise of the youth whose every kiss, every touch had stolen her senses, his fingers entwined in her own, a hand at her back, holding her safe against the breadth of wide shoulders, their bodies touching close. Looking at her as if he could not believe what he was seeing.

His eyes were still that thrilling swirl of grey and green that, for years, had haunted her dreams. To look at his wide, sensuous mouth was to feel his lips angled against hers, feel the heat of his need echoed in the desire pounding through her veins and for a moment, weakly, she leaned into him.

'Chloe...' He breathed her name into her hair, as uncertain as the first time he'd kissed her, as the first time they had made love. The same thrilling tremor rippled through her and for a heartbeat, maybe two, she was that girl again, in his arms, lifting her face to him, inviting more.

And then he said her name again, not with that first rare wonder, but with disbelief written into the frown puckering his forehead.

She was clinging to him, waiting for his kiss, while he was attempting to relate the glossy princess of the sixth form with whom he had fallen in love to the maid turning down his bed.

His confusion brought her to her senses.

James Harrington was living his dream, the one they had shared in grabbed moments of privacy, in the precious, never to be forgotten, stolen half-term week that her parents had thought she was spending with an aristocratic school friend. He'd rented a cottage on the coast. They'd swum in the cold sea, eaten luscious food in the middle of the night, made love in front of the fire, totally consumed by their passion.

Blissful, precious days when they hadn't had to hide, but had lived their dream, planning the life they would have together one day in Paris. A fantasy world where, for a few short days, nothing could touch them.

And then the stick had turned blue.

James had done his best to convince her that he could take care of her and their baby, that they would be together no matter what. She'd wanted to believe him, but that fantasy had died with morning sickness. That was something you couldn't keep secret in the hothouse atmosphere of school. Someone had heard her and ratted her out to matron.

'Chloe?' James kept her hand in his as she took a step back, attempting to reclaim a little dignity.

'No...'

Rage, despair, long hours working three jobs had taken their toll and she was no longer that Chloe. *His* Chloe.

She couldn't bear for him to see her like this and she wrenched her hand away, throwing it up to keep him back as she stepped back towards the door.

'No!' she repeated more forcefully as he took a step towards her.

The fierceness of her rejection stopped him, giving her time to wrench open the door.

'Chloe, wait!'

The uncertainty was gone, now. All doubt.

Ten years older, without the dewy freshness, the gloss, of the girl he'd known, pretending not to know him, to only speak French—he might have hesitated, been left with that disturbed feeling you had when you saw a stranger who looked like someone you once knew.

That might have given her enough time to escape.

But he'd always been Jay to everyone.

James, soft and sweet, was the name she'd used when they were on their own. A stranger would not have clung to him, lips parted, inviting a kiss. No maid would abandon her trolley and run, and she knew that he would come after her, demanding answers that she did not have.

He'd grown up in a hotel, knew his way around behind the scenes; there would be no hiding place and she didn't wait to explain, to change. She just grabbed her coat, bag, boots and made her escape down the narrow lane at the rear of the hotel, the thin soles of her flats slithering on the icy cobbles.

Once in the street, she was quickly swallowed up by the Christmas-shopping crowds laden with glossy carrier bags from the designer stores on the Rue Saint-Honoré, but she didn't slow.

She kept running until she was below ground in the safety of the Metro where she boarded the first train to arrive, pushing into the crush, heart pounding, shivering more with shock than cold, gasping for breath, as the train sped through the dark.

It was early evening and the train had the steamy heat of transport packed with people wanting only to get home to their families, food and warmth after a hard day.

Chloe didn't see them, hear the coughs, the grumbles.

She was lost in the memory of the last time she'd woken in James's arms. His repeated promise that they would be together, that he would be there for her, always. The brief stolen kiss when he'd received a text telling him that he'd been picked to join the cricket team for a grudge match with a rival school on the other side of the county.

It had never occurred to either of them to be suspicious.

There had been no hint of anything other than an ordinary school day until she'd been called to the head's office.

The head wasn't there. Her parents were alone and so, she'd realised, was she. Matron had pretended to believe her diet story, but it was clear that she had not been fooled.

While she had been listening to Miss Kent drone on about Hardy, someone had packed her belongings and within ten minutes of being delivered into the hands of her mother and father she had been driven away from school.

She had been cut off from the moment she'd left the classroom; there had been no way for her to leave a note, a message.

James had known where she lived but even if he'd come after her, he wouldn't have found her. They hadn't taken the road towards their Hampshire estate, or the motorway into London.

Frightened, she had asked her mother where they were going. Her only response had been to hand her a tissue and turn away.

James Harrington, stunned, scarcely able to believe his eyes, his ears, remained rooted to the spot.

He had barely noticed the woman turning down his bed. He was still coming to terms with the sudden turn of events in London. The reappearance of his older brother after seventeen years of silence, the announcement that Hugo was the new owner of the Harrington Park Hotel.

Once he'd recovered from the shock, heard his story, he'd been thrilled that his estranged older brother, Hugo, wanted both him and Sally to be involved in wiping out the bad years when their stepfather Nick Wolfe had been in control. Excited that he wanted them both to help him restore the hotel to the icon it had once been. But his return had dredged up brutal memories. That ghastly Christmas morning when he and Sally had woken up to discover that Hugo was gone, and no one would tell them where he was or when he'd be home.

Their mother had done her best to fill the gap left by his absence, to be there for them. She had even signed the hotel over to Nick, no doubt convinced by him that it would give her more time to spend with her remaining children. The man was an ace manipulator.

The car crash in which she'd died had shattered them both, and Nick Wolfe had been quick to rid himself of the burden of a couple of stepchildren.

It had hit Sally especially hard and her reaction when Hugo had turned up out of the blue had been a release of all that anger, all the pain that had been bottled up inside her.

He'd understood her inability to accept that Hugo had been forced to stay away, to empathise with what he'd been through, but it had been emotionally draining, his nights disturbed by the return of exhausting dream searches down endless corridors for those lost.

His parents.

Hugo.

Chloe and the baby they had made.

She had vanished off the face of the earth ten years ago and when he'd seen her reflection in the window beside him, he had thought for a moment that he was imagining it. That she was a phantom dredged up by those dreams.

Then their eyes had met.

He'd caught her as she'd swayed, felt her breath on his cheek, his lips. Could still feel the warmth of her hand where he'd grasped her fin-

gers. Still, in his mind, feel the warmth of lips
that had, for just a moment, been his to take.

Instead, scarcely able to believe his eyes, he
had hesitated, unsure, and she had run.

Did she believe that he had rejected her?

'Never!'

Jerking himself out of shocked immobility, he
wrenched open the door but wasted seconds had
given Chloe time to disappear.

She wouldn't have waited for the lift and he
raced to the staff stairs, which led straight down
to a part of the hotel that guests never saw. He
was down two flights before reality brought him
crashing to a halt.

If he burst into Housekeeping, chasing a
woman who'd run from him, he knew exactly
what they'd think. Bad enough, but he'd won a
major television show, was the youngest chef
ever to win a Michelin star for L'Étranger, the
restaurant he'd founded on the back of his television fame.

His face had been on the cover of enough lifestyle and food magazines to make him recognis-
able, especially here in Paris where food was
a religion.

He didn't care what they said about him, but
speculation would be all over social media by
morning.

Until he knew why Chloe was working here,

in Housekeeping, he needed to exercise discretion because something was wrong. Badly wrong.

The Forbes Scotts were old money. The kind of people who lived behind a security cordon on their estate when they were in the country. In a penthouse apartment accessible only from a private lift in the city. Who spent their vacations on the private islands owned by their friends.

Powerful, rich as Croesus, they could, as he'd discovered when he'd tried to contact Chloe, throw up a wall of silence as impenetrable as their security systems.

He hadn't seen or heard from her since she'd been whisked away while he'd been on the other side of the county, bored out of his mind, sitting out the game as twelfth man on the sidelines of the pitch.

After all the publicity about the Michelin star he had, for a while, lived in hope that Chloe might walk into L'Étranger one day; take in the clubby atmosphere of the ground floor, order a cocktail, ask to meet the chef. Or maybe arrive for the fine dining on the floor above with friends, a partner...

At least send him a card offering her congratulations.

Something. Anything.

Pie in the sky.

She might have smiled to see his success, perhaps remembered a doomed, youthful passion, but she would have moved on, married someone approved by her parents.

She would definitely not want to have her life complicated by him turning up and demanding answers.

Clearly, whatever had happened in the years since she'd disappeared from school, it couldn't have been that.

Did she marry someone her parents disapproved of? That wouldn't be difficult. She'd warned him how it would be. Money spoke to money and anyone short of a multimillionaire would have been viewed as a fortune hunter.

Did she have a family now?

He leaned back against the wall, swept up in the memory of the anger, the pain of the young man he'd been. He'd had no illusions about the likely outcome of a youthful pregnancy caused by the urgency of their need for one another. His ineptitude.

He pounded a fist into the wall.

Did she think that he'd blame her? She'd warned him what her parents were like, how controlling they were, but with the arrogance of youth he'd dismissed her fears. He'd had the money his father had left him. A pittance compared to her family's wealth, but enough to live the life they had talked about.

He'd promised he would take care of her and their baby. Promised that they would be a family.

He swore as his phone pinged a warning that it was time to leave for his meeting with the chef he hoped to recruit for Harrington's. He turned to walk back up the stairs and paused as something glinted on the steps above him.

He reached out and picked up a piece of crushed silver. It was, or had been, an art deco silver hairpin. He knew that because he'd bought it for Chloe's seventeenth birthday, and it seemed likely that he'd stood on it on his rush down the stairs.

He did not want to leave but Chloe was, for the moment, beyond his reach and time was short if Hugo was to have the hotel open for Christmas Eve.

Louis Joubert was an old friend, but even so it was going to be a hard sell and he had the dramatic temperament to match his flair. He had squeezed in this meeting before starting service and keeping him waiting would not be a good start.

James slipped the piece of silver into his pocket to deal with later.

It was a crazy busy time of year for everyone and he should be in London, in his own kitchen, but he wasn't leaving Paris until he'd talked to Chloe.

CHAPTER TWO

Sally, I've just arrived in Paris and I've seen Chloe! She's working at my hotel as a housekeeper. She ran away when I recognised her. I couldn't follow her and now I have to meet Louis before he starts work. I'll find her tomorrow, try and talk to her then, but I had to tell you. How is Singapore? J x

OMG! What on earth is she doing working as a maid in a hotel? Her family is minted. I'm not surprised she ran. She must have been mortified to have you see her like that. Do be careful, Jay. You'll be ripping a plaster off an old wound for both of you. S x

THERE WAS A second text a few moments later.

Singapore is a lot warmer than Paris, btw. And totally inspiring.

Sally had added a smiley face to her second text, which suggested that she at least was enjoying the break, which after the last few weeks was a relief. But his twin knew Chloe, knew what her disappearance had done to him.

Losing people had been a big part of their lives. It had defined them. Made them into the people they were.

'Jay! I'm sorry to be late. The traffic…'

Lost in the memory of the week that he and Chloe had stolen to be together, Jay was jerked back to the present by Louis's apologetic arrival but it took a moment to gather himself before he stood and greeted his old friend with a hug.

Chloe had told her parents that she would be staying with a school friend for the summer half-term break. No one had cared where he was.

It had been blissfully hot that week and her skin had been silky gold as they'd swum naked in the sea on their last evening, unaware that the clock had already been ticking down on their last moments together.

'No problem, Louis. It's good to see you.'

'Is it? You were far away, my friend,' he said, sitting down. 'I had to say your name twice. Or maybe you are now so grand that you only answer to James?'

'No,' he said quickly. Only two people had ever called him that. His mother and Chloe… 'It's still Jay.' He shook his head. 'I've a lot on my mind. It's a crazy time of year in this business.'

'In any business,' Louis replied, 'but forgive

me for doubting that you were contemplating the deconstruction of a figgy pudding for your Christmas menu. That depth of introspection usually involves a woman.'

Jay managed a smile. 'You have rather more experience in that department than I.'

Louis lifted his hands in a wordless gesture before proving Jay's point by reducing the waitress to a blushing mess with no more than a lift of an eyebrow to gain her attention.

'So? Who is she?' Louis asked, after ordering coffee.

Jay shook his head, but said, 'A girl I knew a long time ago. It was a shock to see her in Paris.'

'A pleasant one?'

'Pleasant?' That was far too bland a word. 'It was something of a bombshell if I'm honest.' He was still struggling to believe it… 'It was a long time ago. We were very young.'

'The bittersweet memory of first love?' Louis's shrug was a masterpiece of Gallic appreciation. 'Your heart is broken, but you become a man.'

'How very French.'

Louis grinned. 'What can I say? The world is full of beautiful women and food is the most seductive of life's pleasures. It gives to all the senses. Scent, taste, touch… Well, I do not need to spell it out for someone who is the master of his art,' he said, his grin fading as he remembered some past pleasure of his own, or maybe pain.

'No…' And Jay was the one reliving that moment when he'd held out a spoon for Chloe to taste some treat he'd made for her. Eyes closed, she had sighed with pleasure as she'd licked it, then melted as he had kissed it off her tongue.

'Why are you wasting time talking to me when you could be with her?' Louis asked, after a long moment when they were both lost in the memory of that first—and for Jay only—love.

'It's complicated,' he said, forcing himself to focus on the reason he was in Paris. 'And pinning you down to this meeting was too difficult—' too important '—for me to bail at the last minute.'

London might be the hottest place to eat right now but Louis was French to his marrow and the Harrington Park Hotel had been on the slide for years.

He'd promised Hugo he would find him a chef capable of bringing one of the fabled Michelin stars to the restaurant. He'd worked with Louis in Paris when they were both at the bottom of the ladder, fighting to be noticed, and he was top of a very short list, but James had no illusions that persuading him to take the necessary leap of faith was going to be a piece of patisserie.

Tomorrow he would find Chloe, talk to her, find out what had happened all those years ago. Find out why she was working as a maid in a hotel. Why she had never contacted him.

He scarcely dared believe that she would be free. Had there been a ring on her finger?

That brief touch was seared into his brain and, despite Sally's warning, he was clinging to the edge of hope.

Aware that Louis was regarding him thoughtfully, he launched into details of Hugo's experience in running a highly successful chain of boutique hotels in New York, before outlining his brother's ambitious plans for the Harrington Park Hotel.

'So, what is your vision for the restaurant?'

Louis's very casual question did not fool Jay. As he'd hoped, the chef's entire body language had sharpened at the mention of a New York connection. The possibility that London might be the stepping stone to even bigger things.

He'd cast his line, now he needed to give it a little tug.

'It won't be my vision, Louis,' he said. 'It will be yours.'

'I would have total control?' he asked, finally losing the casual pose. 'Surely you will be Chef Patron at your family hotel?'

'The hotel is Hugo's passion, Louis. I'm delighted that it's back in family hands and I'm happy to help where I can, but I have my own ambitions.'

'More restaurants?'

'I'm working on a couple of ideas,' he admitted, 'but in the immediate future I'm going to be writing a food column for one of the lifestyle magazines and I'm working with a publisher on a book adapted from the blog I've been writing since the beginning of my journey.'

'Your blog…' Louis raised a hand in admiration. 'It reads like a love letter to food.'

Close… He'd begun the blog that first winter in Paris, after he'd fled London. It had been a way of talking to Chloe, telling her where he was, what he was doing without invoking the wrath of her family.

'You are going to be very busy, my friend.'

He'd spent two years in the city before getting his break on a television show. His shrug, as Gallic as anything Louis could throw at him, suggested that time was not a problem, but he wasn't about to confess to the total lack of a social life.

It wasn't for the lack of opportunity. He was driven to succeed, to show the world, to show Nick Wolfe, Chloe's parents—as if they cared— that he was worthy of their respect.

Hugo and Sally were equally compelled. It was their legacy.

Taking the hint, Louis moved back to the purpose of their meeting. 'Who else are you seeing while you're in Paris?'

It was time to reel him in.

'I told Hugo I would find him a *chef de cuisine* who would give him a star within twelve months. The competition in London is red hot right now but I believe you are the man for the job, Louis. The question is, are you up for that challenge?'

He didn't wait for an answer but swiftly laid out the terms of the very generous package Hugo was offering and, while Louis was still taking that in, said, 'When can you be in London to start recruiting your team?'

'You are that sure I'll say yes?' Jay didn't respond. 'It's a big step, leaving everything here.' When he still said nothing, Louis said, 'You did it when you were far younger than me.'

'I had nothing to lose, everything to gain.' For him the move had been an escape, a chance to leave behind everything that reminded him of the people he'd lost. 'This is a rare opportunity, Louis. A chance to make your mark internationally, but time is of the essence and I will need an answer by tomorrow.'

'I'll have to give notice.'

'Speaking from experience, I think you'll find that a chef with his mind elsewhere will not be encouraged to linger.' He relaxed a little, sure now that he had his man. 'Don't you have a *sous chef* stepping on your heels? Someone who is always coming up with ideas for new dishes, encouraging you to take a day off? Go on vacation?'

Louis responded with a rueful smile. 'A precociously talented brat who reminds me of you. I feel his hot breath on my neck every day.'

'Then this is his big moment as well as yours.'

'Maybe. He'll be cheaper than me and times are tough. I'll talk to my boss after service. Whatever happens, I'll call you tomorrow with my answer.'

'By midday.' He was reassured by the fact that Louis wasn't prepared to walk out on his commitments, but there was a time pressure. 'Hugo plans to open the hotel with a party on Christmas Eve. He's going to recreate what was always a special event for guests, staff, family…'

He could still see his father lifting Sally up so that she could hang her new decoration high on the huge tree in the entrance hall. Could still feel the prickle, the smell of the pine as he hung his own ornament. His mother's smiling face as she watched Hugo do the same before the switch was thrown and the tree was lit up in a shimmer of a thousand tiny white lights…

'That's pushing it, Jay. Creating and testing an entirely new menu takes time.'

'What? Oh, yes, but you won't be on your own. My staff will offer you every assistance until you've had the time to recruit your own team.' The Harrington siblings were reclaiming part of their lives they had thought lost for ever and it had to be a success. 'But if you're half the chef I believe you to be, you'll have a notebook full of ideas.'

'Thank you, Jay.' Louis stood up and offered his hand. 'I know that this is a huge opportunity and I appreciate your faith in me. If I'm released, I won't let you down.'

'How long will you need to wrap up things here?'

'There is nothing to keep me. My mother will take care of subletting my flat.'

'You can stay at the hotel until you've had time to find somewhere,' he said, leaving cash on the table and walking with Louis to the door. 'You've met Sally?'

'She came to visit when you were working here. You are twins, yes?'

Jay nodded. Twins, but she had been so much more fragile, battered by a series of devastating losses. It had been down to him to take care of her when their stepfather had shown his true colours, changing their status at St Mary's from day pupils to boarders when the ink was barely dry on their mother's death certificate.

And then he'd left her, too, walking out of school when he'd discovered that Chloe was gone.

There had only been staff at Chloe's family estate in Hampshire, at the flat in London, none of whom had been talking. He hadn't known if he would have been allowed to return to school. He hadn't gone back, but instead had begged a job in the kitchen of a hotelier who had known his father while he'd continued to search for her.

He was just minutes older than his sister, but at times it felt like years.

'Sally is an interior designer now,' he said. 'Very talented. Hugo has asked her to take on the restyling of the hotel and she's in Singapore seeking inspiration. No doubt you will want to work with her so that the dining room and menu are a match.'

'You're thinking fusion?' Louis asked, with a frown.

'I'm thinking international with inspiring vegetarian and vegan dishes. Will that be a problem?'

'It is the way the world is moving,' Louis agreed. 'I have a great many ideas that I haven't been able to introduce to a restaurant serving classic French cuisine. Many inspired by you. How long are you staying in Paris?'

That had always depended on whether Louis

accepted the offer. It was a busy time of year and he was needed in his own kitchen, but he wouldn't leave until he'd talked to Chloe.

'I'll take the chance to look at a few restaurants while I'm here,' he said. 'Is there anywhere interesting that you would recommend?'

They paused in the doorway, while Louis suggested several places, then put a hand on his arm. 'Life is more than work, Jay. Forgive me, but you look like a man who needs a holiday. Paris is a city made for love. Find your girl, revisit old times.'

Jay watched him stride away. Louis was right. He was tired, drained by an excess of emotional angst, late-night meetings with Hugo and Sally, but he knew he wouldn't sleep. Instead of returning to the hotel, he began to walk, oblivious to the cold, pausing only to watch the lights dancing on the Eiffel Tower as a bell in a nearby church tower chimed the hour.

Chloe stirred as the train stopped, looked up and, realising where she was, pushed through the crush to get off. There were messages on her phone from Augustin, who owned the bistro where she worked in the evening, pleading with her to come in as soon as she could.

Her head was pounding and all she wanted to do was go home, curl up in bed and pull the covers over her head but Augustin had been good to her and she couldn't let him down. Besides, there was no time to think when she was serving; force of habit kept a smile on her face and just now she needed anything that would keep her from thinking about all she'd lost.

James. Their baby…

Seeing him brought back all that pain and for a moment she was so overwhelmed by grief that she clung to the stair rail while people pushed by.

Someone stopped to ask if she needed help, but she shook her head, forced her legs to move.

Back on the pavement, out of the shelter of the Metro, she was caught by a fit of shivering. Shock as much as the cold stinging her eyes that were wet with rare tears. She blinked them away as she reached the bistro, grateful for the warmth and the relieved welcome of Augustin who, rushed off his feet, didn't care that she was late, only that she had arrived.

She swallowed a couple of painkillers for her head, dealt with hair that had come loose in her haste and realised that she'd lost the silver pin that kept it in place. The silver pin that James had bought her for her seventeenth birthday.

That was the moment that she gave into the tears, sinking onto the floor as they ran, unchecked, down her face.

'Chloe? Are you okay?' There was a tap on

the door and when she didn't answer, Augustin opened it. *'Chérie…what is it?'*

She scrambled to her feet, dashing away the tears. 'Nothing. I'm upset because I lost something precious. Stupid. I'll be right there…'

He looked doubtful.

'Really. Just give me a minute.'

He nodded and a couple of minutes later she was in her apron, apologising as she took orders from impatient diners. This was what she did now. What she was.

The money wasn't great, but she worked hard for the tips, saving every cent, hoping one day to create a future for herself. A life where no one could dictate what she did, what she thought, who she loved.

But she was on edge; every time the door opened behind her she twitched, half expecting to hear a familiar voice.

'Mademoiselle…?'

Recalled to attention by a diner, she forced a smile. *'Poulet fermier,'* she said, repeating the last item, just to prove that she had been listening, took the rest of the order and then went to the bar to collect their drinks.

'Are you okay, Chloe?' the barman asked as he removed the cap from a bottle of beer.

'It's been a long day.' She stretched her aching neck. 'We're short-staffed at the hotel. It's not just here that I'm doing the work of two.'

But not tomorrow. Tomorrow was Sunday and the bistro was closed. And as for the hotel…

She didn't know how long James would be staying, but he would be waiting for her and she wasn't going anywhere near it until she was sure that he'd checked out.

Jay gave up on sleep long before it was light, but there was already a text from Louis confirming that he would take the job and, in view of the urgency, would be leaving for London that morning.

He responded with pleasure and not a little relief and, despite the early hour, called Hugo to give him the good news.

'Thanks, Jay. That's a big item crossed off the list. Are you catching the early Eurostar?'

He should get back to London, but his own *sous chef* was more than capable of holding the fort and he couldn't leave until he'd found Chloe, talked to her.

'There are a few things I need to do here,' he said, 'but tell Louis to call my office if he needs help in recruiting staff. We have a waiting list of really good people I'd give a job to in a heartbeat if I had an opening.'

There was a moment of silence while Hugo

digested that, but all he said was, 'Thanks. I'll see you when you get back.'

He wasn't leaving the room until he'd seen Chloe, so, after a quick shower, he ordered croissants and coffee from room service. It was still early, but he hung a 'make up my room' sign on the door, took his laptop to the desk, out of sight of the door, and settled down to wait.

It was late afternoon before there was a tap on the door, a call of, 'Housekeeping.' It wasn't Chloe. Not exactly a surprise.

He'd hoped she might, once she'd thought about it, decide to face him, but if that was the case, she wouldn't have come here. She would have called him through the hotel switchboard and arranged to meet somewhere neutral.

She hadn't done that, and someone else was working her floor, so she had to be avoiding him.

The housekeeper seemed surprised to see him there, but with a wave of his hand he indicated that she should carry on, waiting until she was pulling back the bed before, very casually, asking, 'Where's Chloe today?'

'Chloe?' Her expression was blank.

'The English girl who was working this floor yesterday. She was at school with my sister,' he said, which was perfectly true.

'Oh?' Her cautious response suggested doubt, but he pressed on, as if he hadn't noticed.

'Is it her day off?'

She shrugged. 'No. She called in sick today. Everyone has the flu.'

'I'm sorry to hear that. I hoped to catch her before I leave.' The girl stopped fussing with the pillow and waited. He noted the name on her staff badge and said, 'I'm in Paris recruiting staff for my family hotel in London, Julianne. After I saw Chloe, I texted my sister—' which was also true '—and she wants to offer her a job.' Not true, but he didn't have time to mess around with complicated explanations. 'I don't suppose you have her telephone number? Or, better still, her address?' She was unlikely to answer a call from a number she didn't know. 'If she's sick, Sally would want me to make sure she's okay.'

'They'll have it in the office,' Julianne pointed out.

He pulled a face. 'A bit awkward asking them for it. Under the circumstances.'

Another shrug, but this time there was only one meaning. A fifty-euro note found its way into her hand and a minute later he had what he wanted.

Aware that he had run the risk of exposure, he shouldered the backpack that contained his laptop and change of clothes, asked the receptionist to call him a taxi to take him to the Gare du Nord, and checked out.

At the railway station he bought flowers and took the Metro to the outskirts of Paris. It was getting dark by the time he reached the shabby cobbled street where Chloe lived. Her apartment was at the top of the house and, heart sinking, he climbed five flights of cold, cheerless stairs with damp running down walls that looked as if they hadn't seen a lick of paint in half a century.

There was no response to his knock, but a chink of light showed under a large gap at the bottom of the door.

'Chloe!' he called, knocking again.

Nothing.

Angry now, he raised his voice. 'Come on, Chloe. I'm not leaving, so you might as well let me in.'

CHAPTER THREE

CHLOE LEANED AGAINST the door, fighting the desperate urge to open it. To see James one more time.

She had done everything to try and shut down her brain but, ever since she'd seen him reflected in that window, her memory had been running a loop of the time they had been together, replaying every moment she had spent with him.

She had come close to calling the hotel to speak to him more than half a dozen times, telling herself that it had been cowardly to run, that he would have questions.

Or maybe not.

James had been shocked to see her but, unlike her, he'd achieved what he'd talked about, dreamed about. He had an exciting and successful career. She doubted that he had more than a fleeting memory of a youthful infatuation and, as she'd watched his rise, she'd told herself that she was content. That she wanted him to be fulfilled, happy.

Seeing him so unexpectedly had shattered that

image of selflessness. She was furious with him for being the guest in a luxury hotel, while she was the one making his bed.

Alone in her miserable one-room apartment, she wanted to lash out, scream at him, tell him what she'd suffered, but with him standing on the other side of the door all she could think about was that spring and summer when, for the briefest moment, she had been happy.

'Please, Chloe…' This time he was begging and, unable to help herself, she turned the key and opened the door.

James straightened as if he had been leaning against it until he heard the key turn. There were dark shadows beneath his eyes as if, like her, a sleepless night had been spent remembering…

For a moment they just stood in silence, looking at each other. Then he reached out, grazed her cheek with his cold fingers and, without thinking, she leaned into his hand like a kitten seeking comfort.

He drew her close, so that her head was against his chest, against his beating heart, and her arms, with nothing else to do, encircled a chest broader than she remembered.

He took a step forward, taking her with him as he kicked the door shut. The flowers he'd been holding hit the floor, a bag slipped from his shoulder and they were in each other's arms without a word being spoken, clinging to one another as if they would never let go.

After for ever, he leaned back, cradling her face between his hands as he looked at her. As she looked at him.

He brushed a tear from her cheek with the pad of his thumb, kissed away another, then she was tasting the salt as his lips found hers.

It had been a long time since she'd been kissed, felt desired, beautiful. She'd dreamed of this moment, imagined how it would be when the lost years fell away and she'd be that girl on the cusp of her seventeenth birthday, melting in the arms of a boy who made her feel like a princess.

This was nothing like that fantasy.

They had spent nearly a year getting to know one another in the most intimate of ways. James knew all the sweet spots, and she groaned with pleasure as he deepened the kiss, her limbs liquefying as cold fingers stroked the back of her neck, slid beneath her sweater to cup her breast, teasing her already rigid nipple with the tip of his thumb.

There was nothing but hot, desperate need as he stoked the heat and she was with him every step of the way as, shedding clothes with every step, he backed her across the room until she was pinned against the wall. Abandoning her lips, he took her breast, the nipple now achingly hard against her bra, into his mouth.

She cried out as he sucked hard, a shout of triumph that could have been heard over the bells of Notre Dame, urging him on as his hand breached leggings, underwear, to seek out the hot silky ache between her legs.

Desperate, weak with longing, she dug her fingers into his shoulders as he raised his head and looked straight into her eyes as he stroked her to a peak of pleasure. Watched as she fell apart beneath his touch until, at the perfect moment, he drove his fingers deep inside her to deliver a shattering release.

Still shaking with the aftershock, she grabbed handfuls of his tee shirt and pulled it over his head. She wanted to touch him, taste him, feel his skin next to hers. Give him what he'd just given her and more.

She pressed her lips, her tongue, against his chest, tasting him, her hands busy with button and zip as she backed him towards the bed and he tumbled across it.

What followed was raw, brutally intense, utterly consuming and afterwards Chloe lay with her heart pounding, her breasts crushed against a rock-hard chest that was hairier than she remembered, their legs entangled in the intimate confines of her narrow bed, as she came down from the high of a tumultuous climax.

Only one word had been spoken since James had walked through the door. 'Wait…' as he had grabbed his trousers from her hands. Protecting her. Protecting them both.

A hard lesson learned.

Now the only sound was of them catching their breath as they looked at each other with the dazed expression of two people who'd just had the sky fall in on them. As the reality of what had just happened began to dawn on them.

On her.

She had just had rip-your-clothes-off sex with a man she hadn't seen for ten years. She didn't do that. Ever…

Well, not since the time when, despite all the plans they had made, she had, deep down, known that their future would never happen and, in a moment of desperation, despair, had thrown herself at him.

As a teenager it had been stupid. And they had both paid a price for that.

As an adult that total loss of control was embarrassment on the Richter scale even with the protection.

What had she been thinking?

She looked across the broad chest, to the stubble of beard that was new. The easy answer was that she hadn't been thinking, but that would be wrong. She'd been thinking and thinking and remembering for the best part of twenty-four hours.

Thinking about every moment, every touch, her body vibrating from thoughts that refused to be shut out. The sight of him had lit the blue touchpaper and, when she'd touched him, it had gone off like New Year's Eve.

At least it was the same man—the *only* man.

She could console herself with the fact that it was about him rather than simple lust. But what did you say after ten years?

James turned his head and said, 'Hello.'

That was it. It was that simple?

Not simple.

She had to force her response through a throat constricted by a mangle of emotions. Not the embarrassment, the awkwardness, but joy, wonder, to know everything she had clung to was real, true; that her passion for James was as intense, immediate, overwhelming as it had been when she was seventeen.

'Hello.' The word was barely audible, but James smiled and shifted his arm so that he could put it around her shoulders, pull her closer and for a moment she could close her eyes and imagine that she was a teenager again and in love.

Then, James said, 'We're going to need a bigger bed.'

In spite of the emotional turmoil whirling around her head, she let out a shout of laughter.

He'd said the exact same words one evening when they were supposed to be revising for a biology exam and had opted for the practical.

'You remembered,' he said, grinning.

'How could I forget? *Jaws* was your favourite movie and when I didn't get the reference, you insisted I watch it with you. It scared me so much I...' She stopped as she remembered exactly what she'd done to make him turn off the movie. 'So, what's your favourite film now you're a famous chef with a Michelin star?' she asked, before he could go there.

'It will always be *Jaws*...' He raised a hand to briefly cradle her cheek. 'Are you hungry?'

She had been starving it seemed, but not for food. The mention of it, however, brought her crashing back to reality and she yelped as she caught sight of the clock.

'I'm going to be late for work!' she said, wriggling free of his legs, his arms as she tumbled out of bed.

'Work?'

He sat up, combing his fingers through hair she had so thoroughly tousled. She dragged her eyes away, opened drawers looking for clean underwear but the bed squeaked as he stood up. The room was small; all it took was a step and she could feel the heat of his body at her back.

'I thought you called in sick today.'

'No...' She turned to face him. 'I said it was a family emergency, but I work evenings as a waitress at a bistro.'

James looked around, taking in the tiny studio apartment. The kitchen scarcely more than a cupboard. The place in the corner where the rain had come through the roof and the wallpaper she'd put up to make it feel more like home was stained and peeling away.

'It takes two jobs to live like this?'

'Three. I do some cleaning work when I can get it. Paris is expensive and I won't be paid for the day I missed at the hotel.'

'They can't do that,' he protested.

'It's agency work. They can do whatever they like.'

'I'll cover it...' The words died in his mouth as he realised how that must sound. 'We have to talk, Chloe.'

'There's nothing to talk about.' She needed to take a shower but, as she turned away, church bells began to ring. 'Oh... It's Sunday...'

'All day.'

'I...' She shook her head. 'I don't know whether I'm coming or going.'

'I think we both know the answer to that,' he said. 'Loud enough for the neighbours to hear.'

Blushing furiously, she ducked around him and shut herself in the shower. The pressure was abysmal and the water lukewarm or she'd have stayed under it until he gave up and left.

Fat chance of that. He wasn't going anywhere until he had answers to all the questions that must have been burning a hole in his brain for years.

She was going to have to talk to him and the sooner it was done, the sooner she could get back to reality.

When she emerged, still a bit damp around the edges, but dressed, the kettle was on and James was fastening the buttons on his shirt. One was hanging on a thread. As he attempted to fasten it, it came away in his hand and he looked at it for a moment, and they were both remembering the moment when she'd tugged at it in the frantic race to get out of their clothes.

'Give it to me,' she said. 'I'll sew it back on for you.' Because if he didn't stop looking at her like that there was only one hunger that would be satisfied. If they were going to talk, they needed to get out of this room. 'And in answer to your question, yes, I'm hungry.'

'I've got a few recommendations. I'll see if I

can get a table somewhere,' he said, putting the button in her hand and shrugging out of his shirt.

The boy she'd loved had been a slender, graceful youth but the years had given his body strength, power, maturity. He was everything she had loved and more and it took every ounce of self-control not to wrap herself around him, fall back into bed and let the world go hang.

Self-control was something she'd learned the hard way. She'd had years to work on blocking those memories. Keeping those feelings at arm's length. Easily resisting the temptation to accept temporary relief when it had been offered. Or so she'd imagined.

Easy to resist when there was only one man who could give her what she wanted. The barriers had come tumbling down when it was that man standing in front of her.

Once, one time…

She'd spent the few minutes in the shower reminding herself of all the reasons that it could not happen again. Shoring up the barriers. Even so, it was a relief when he pulled on his sweater while she sewed on the button.

He was cold, not taking pity on her, she told herself as she hooked her sewing basket out from under the bed and searched for a needle and matching thread.

'Tea or coffee?' he asked as the kettle boiled.

'T-tea, please,' she replied, sitting on the edge of the bed, concentrating hard to thread the needle with hands that were not quite steady.

His hand fastened over hers, stilling the shake before he took the needle from her and threaded it.

He handed it back without a word, made tea in two mugs, set them on the bedside table and sat beside her.

'How long will it take you to pack?' he asked.

'Pack?' She jabbed herself with the needle, leaving a tiny spot of blood on his shirt.

He took her hand, looked at it, and said, 'You'll live, but I'm not sure you're up to that.'

He took the shirt from her, swiftly stitched the button in place, and by the time he'd returned the needle to the spool and pulled the shirt back on, she had almost regained control over her breathing.

'I'm not going anywhere,' she said.

'You can't stay here.'

Yes… Yes, she could. She had to send him on his way. Convince him somehow that what happened was not important. She took a breath…

'I'm sorry, James. That was a fun trip down memory lane but don't let's get carried away.'

'Look at me, Chloe.'

His voice was low, cobweb soft, but it had an undeniable force and she obeyed without considering the foolishness of such a move. She was shivering and his warmth was tempting her to lean into him, press her lips in the curve of his neck where it met his shoulder. Trembling with the need to put her arms around him, slide her hands down his body, feel the contraction of his muscles, the leap of his response to her touch.

She lowered her lashes so as not to be drawn in by the intensity of his grey-green eyes, but his voice was insistent.

'Look me in the eyes, Chloe, and tell me again that was just a bit of fun. That it's something you do every time a man knocks on your door with a bunch of flowers in his hand.'

She whimpered, a wordless denial that betrayed her and he reached out, lifted her chin so that she was looking directly into his eyes.

'Do you think I didn't look for you?' he asked. 'That I didn't climb the walls of your family estate? Try every way to get past the security at the London penthouse? Contact all of your friends in an effort to find you?'

She swallowed down the ache in her throat, knowing how that would have gone.

'I had dogs set on me, a beating from security guards—'

'They hurt you?'

'They made their point quite thoroughly, but that wasn't the worst.' She closed her eyes as if she could blot out whatever was coming. 'The worst was the summons to Nick Wolfe's office where a solicitor informed me that if I didn't stop "harassing" you, your family and friends, they would go to court and take out a restraining order. Can you imagine how much my stepfather enjoyed being a witness to that humiliation?'

'You weren't harassing me!'

'I was harassing everyone in pursuit of you.'

'I'm so sorry…'

'I don't want your pity. I want you, Chloe. I've never stopped wanting you and what just happened, happened to both of us. Come back to London with me.'

'London?' She shook her head. 'No…'

His hand opened to cradle her cheek. She had longed for this moment, yearned for the moment when he would hold her, tell her that the nightmare was over and that they would be together.

It was wrong, she knew that it was never going to be over but, weakly, she surrendered to the warmth of his arms and he drew her close.

'I never stopped believing that one day you would get in touch, Chloe. I understood that you couldn't be with me. I just wanted to know that you were okay.'

This was okay. Being held close, being loved…

'Where have you been all this time?' he asked.

'I was sick for a long time, in a clinic—'

He stiffened, drew back to look at her. 'Sick?'

'In my head. After they took our baby.'

And this time, when his arms tightened around her, he held her so close that she could scarcely breathe. She knew that pain; a stab through the heart that no words could ever heal.

'I knew,' he said. 'I always knew they would insist on a termination, but somewhere, deep down, I carried an image of you together.'

She pulled back, looked up at him. His cheeks were wet and, as she wiped her fingers across them, he shivered. For a moment she was tempted to tell him what had really happened, but then he would be burdened with her pain, too.

'I'm sorry, James.'

'Don't apologise to me. I'm the one who messed up. I should have been with you.'

'There was nothing you could have done.'

'I could have tried. If I'd known where you were, I would have come for you. Done anything…'

'Do you think I didn't want to tell you, James? To call your voicemail just to hear your voice? When I was free—'

'Free?'

'Better. When I had recovered,' she corrected herself carefully, 'the situation was made very clear to me. A reputation is a fragile thing, James. If I tried to contact you in any way it would not just be your life in the crusher, but Sally's too, and she had suffered enough.'

'Your parents were that afraid of us being together?'

'We were too young to know what we were doing.' She heard herself trot out words that had been repeated over and over. Gently, coaxingly, with increasing irritation at her stubbornness. Hated them but knew in her heart that they were true.

'Maybe we were,' he said, with an angry gesture at their surroundings, 'but I think we would have done better than this.'

'Would we? Seventeen years old with a baby? Would you be where you are now?' she demanded, feeding off his anger. 'My parents had plans for me, and they didn't include a boy with no family.'

Anger was easier. It was the glue that had held her together, kept her putting one foot in front of the other as she'd refused the soft words, the temptation to accept a comfortable life in return for becoming a coroneted breeding cow...

His body snapped away from hers and cold air filled the gap as he took a long slow look around the apartment, lingering on the crumbling ceiling where the rain regularly came through, and then back at her.

'I may not have a family that can trace its ancestors back to Adam, but some people are more interested in creating something new than looking back at the past.'

'I'm not condoning—' she began, but he wasn't done.

'We may not have had wealth or status in the way your family see it, but there was a trust set up by our grandfather to pay for our education, a substantial inheritance from my grandmother. We would have been young, with a baby, and I'm not fooling myself that it would have been easy, but we wouldn't have been living in a cold room with a leaking roof.'

'You don't understand—'

'What's to understand, Chloe?'

'That it was never about the money.' She sank onto the bed. 'It was about ambition. Much to Father's irritation he could never find a link to the Stuarts so he couldn't actually trace his family back to Adam and hence God—'

'Well, that must have been a blow.'

'But it does go back to one of the barons that came over with the Conqueror.'

'You're serious…' He sat beside her, denting the mattress so that she was tipped towards him. She should move, but the struggle to escape the tilt of the mattress would just make things worse so she stayed very still. 'So why doesn't your father have a title?'

She shrugged. Her shoulder rubbed against his, soaking in his warmth… 'The family straddled both sides in the civil war,' she said quickly. 'The older brother was a Royalist and lost everything. The younger had been close to Cromwell and was lucky to keep his head at the Restoration.'

'And yet they have prospered.'

'They were fast learners. Keep out of politics. Follow the money…

'My father was offered a knighthood for services to charity but considered it beneath him. A bauble for actors and pop stars. He wanted his grandson to have a real title.'

'A real title? How did he imagine that was going to happen?'

'You've heard the expression "a marriage has been arranged…"?'

'What?' He frowned, shook his head. 'No.' Then, when she didn't say anything and he realised that she was serious, 'You have got to be kidding. That's medieval.'

'Not even close. It was still very much part of the deal at the end of the nineteenth century when the British aristocracy was saved from penury by the arrival of American heiresses in search of a title.'

'We've moved on from *Downton Abbey*, Chloe.'

'Not as far as you'd think. I was signed up for the gig when I was still in my pram. The present earl went to school with my father. That's what schools like St Mary's and Eton are for, James. Making useful friendships. Connections with influence and money.'

'I don't believe I'm hearing this.'

'Believe it. The earl was invited to be my god-father. It may have started out as one of those half-joking "Wouldn't it be perfect?" conversations over the font—"My lad, your girl" sort of thing—but the seed was sown and when the earl made some bad financial choices, I became the bail-out option.'

'The boy had no say in this?'

'I imagine he saw it as his duty. The upkeep of a stately pile costs money and marrying it is the family business.'

'Did you know about that? Before we…?' His gesture filled in the gap.

'Theoretically,' she admitted, 'but it was like some pantomime story that had nothing to do with me.'

'Pantomime is right, and it's been ten years, Chloe. I doubt your aristocrat is still hanging onto the glass slipper.'

She shook her head, desperately trying to make him see. 'My family thinks in centuries and you'd be amazed how patient a man can be when there's a fortune at stake.'

'He's still hoping you'll go back?'

'I have no idea what he thinks, but he hasn't married. I have no doubt that my family know where I am, how I live, and are hoping that a really bad winter will finally bring me to my senses.'

James let out a huff of frustration. 'What kind of man is that entitled? And I'm not talking about a coronet. You're an adult, Chloe. No one can force you into a marriage that you don't want.'

'There is no force. The pressures are more subtle than that.' She managed a shrug. 'It's all about duty to the family.'

She raised an eyebrow at his emphatic response.

'I'm sorry, but duty? Really? What about their duty to you? What about love?'

'In their eyes they were doing what was best for me, James. I'd have been the envy of every girl at St Mary's, including your sister.'

He shook his head. 'I'm astonished, under the circumstances, that you were allowed to go to a mixed boarding school.'

'My mother was a boarder at St Mary's. She told my father that the connections, the friendships, I made there would set me up for the future. That was something my father understood. Their marriage was…'

'Arranged?'

'"Carefully managed" was the phrase she used. People with a lot of money tend to be cautious about letting outsiders near enough to get their hands on it. Maybe she wanted to give me the chance to have a little fun before I settled down to duty.'

'Was that all I was?' he asked. 'Your bit of "fun"?'

'No!' She shrugged. 'Maybe. We were very young. If I hadn't become pregnant…' The denial died on her lips and her fingers twitched, wanting to touch him just one more time.

'It might have burned itself out?'

She dug her nails into her palms. 'Yes,' she lied.

'Then I'm to blame for this.' A sweep of his arm took in the room, while his eyes didn't leave her.

'No!' She took a slow, steadying breath and forced herself to look straight into his eyes. 'No, James. We were both there that day. Bad things happened but they were not your fault. I walked away from my family and now I'm asking you to leave and forget you ever saw me.'

'You think I could forget this?' he demanded, standing up without warning so that she had to grab onto the edge of the bed to stop herself from tumbling sideways. 'Do you think I could forget anything that happened between us? I know you were scared but I would have taken care of you.' When she didn't answer, he said, 'Maybe a termination was easier—'

'No!' The denial brought her to her feet.

She'd always thought that it would be easier for him to believe that there had been no baby, that what she'd done was a burden she had to bear alone, but he had a right to know the truth. 'Never… My parents wanted it, but she was all I had…'

'She?'

The silence was thick in the room and she was struggling to breathe.

'She?' he rapped out.

'There was no termination. We had a little girl, James. I called her Eloise…'

CHAPTER FOUR

THE COLOUR DRAINED from James's face. 'A little girl?' he repeated. 'We have a daughter?'

'I held her for a few minutes after she was born. She had a mop of brown hair just like yours, big eyes. She was so beautiful.'

'Was!'

'Is…' she said quickly. 'I imagine her some days.'

Every day, every waking hour…

'I see this bright, happy little girl who looks a lot like Sally, with parents who love her, who will always put her first, listen to her dreams…'

He grasped her arms, bringing her back from her fantasy.

'Where is she, Chloe?'

She shook her head. 'I don't know. My father finally agreed to let me have my baby but only if I signed adoption papers before she was born.'

'Agreed? That wasn't his decision to make.' He dragged fingers through his hair. 'Is what he did even legal?'

'I don't know. I was alone, isolated from anyone I knew, and I would have agreed to anything to save our little girl.' There were tears pouring down her own cheeks now. 'I didn't believe, once she was born, once they'd seen her, held her, that they would force me to go through with it. That they would be able to go through with it.' She swallowed. 'My mother might have weakened but my father sent her away before Eloise was born. He never had any intention of letting emotion get in the way of his plans. I was holding her, but I fell asleep and when I woke, our daughter was gone.'

James opened his mouth, closed it again, unable to speak.

'Afterwards, once I understood that I would never see our baby again, I had a kind of breakdown.'

'How did they explain that to the earl?'

'As far as the world was concerned, I was at a finishing school here in France.'

'But you were in a clinic?' His eyes continued to drill into her brain for long seconds until she shivered and he pulled off his sweater, dropped it over her head and, taking her arms one at a time, fed them into the sleeves as if she were a child, before tugging it down over her body.

She wanted him to hold her, to warm her, to tell her that he understood, but instead he took a phone from his trouser pocket.

'I have to get you out of here,' he said, scrolling through his contacts, his own hand shaking. 'Start packing.'

'No. I can't go to London with you,' she said, turning away to rescue the flowers that had dropped, unheeded, to the floor, abandoned in their frantic need for each other.

Her heart turned over as she saw that they were white roses. The same gorgeous fat buds that had been delivered to her on her seventeenth birthday. Red would have raised eyebrows, and questions, but the staff had assumed that they were from her mother...

She had long ago learned to wall up her feelings, memories, but that survival technique had been obliterated in the heat of passion and now, as she breathed in the scent of the roses, it took every ounce of that hard-won self-control to force down an emotional torrent that threatened to overwhelm her.

Every instinct was to bury her face in the blooms, to tell James that she loved him, just as she had when the world was new, and anything had seemed possible.

She had given him her heart, along with everything else, unreservedly when they were young. She had just done it again, but he must never know that because this wasn't a new beginning.

She had known what her parents had planned

for her and she should never have allowed herself to become involved with him. To put him at risk.

There could never be a new beginning.

James had moved on, was living the life he had planned, and this had to be an end.

The goodbye they'd never had a chance to say.

She drew on all her strength and, saving the self-indulgent pity party for later, she put the flowers in a jug, added water and set them on a table under the window.

'Thank you for these,' she said, with the professionally bright voice she used with customers at the bistro. 'They are lovely.'

Jay watched as she riffled the petals of one of the roses, just as she had when he'd bought them for her once before. Nothing had changed. The heat, the passion. Nothing, and yet everything, and he understood that she was distancing herself from him, sending him away. Doing what she thought was best for him.

There were so many questions he wanted to ask her. Questions he'd blocked out in the hours of practising basic kitchen skills, soaking up knowledge, honing a natural gift until he'd got his big break on a television competition for young professional chefs.

Questions that had been running through his head ever since Chloe had run from his hotel room.

They had been wiped from his mind, ceased to matter as they'd reached for one another, re-connecting, filling the emotional and physical void as, for one shining moment, she'd come into his arms and ten missing years had been blown away in an explosion of passion.

And then, while he was still floating in a state of blissful delusion that the world was, finally, the right way up, the barrier had come back up and she was running again. Not from him, but to protect him. When he should be protecting her.

She had chosen to live in a cold, damp walk-up that was too small to swing a cat in—that no self-respecting cat would tolerate—rather than live in comfort with parents who, not content with stealing their daughter from him, had threatened him and his family. Because that kind of adoption could not be legal. One of his colleagues had adopted and she had been on ten-terhooks for months, in case the mother changed her mind…

They had recognised the threat. Young as he was, determined as he'd been to find her, they had been afraid that if he found out what they'd done he would have talked to a lawyer.

That was what the threats had been about.

He was safe enough, but Chloe was different.

She was living well below the radar, but it was hard to hide these days, especially from people with friends in high places and a bottomless purse, and she was an heiress on a grand scale.

Her father might have disinherited her, but it wasn't that easy. She was their daughter and would have a legal claim on their estate, as would any children she might bear to some man who did not have the Forbes Scott seal of approval.

She might refuse to play by their rules, but they would want to know where she was, what she was doing and who she was doing it with.

His reappearance would be their worst nightmare.

It wasn't the cold draught whistling through the gaps around the window that sent the shiver up his spine. Her parents had been coldly ruthless with Chloe when they had discovered she was pregnant.

It was clear, from the little she'd said, that the loss had come close to destroying her, that she had been confined to some kind of sanatorium for months, maybe longer.

He had been unable to help her, protect her back then, but guilt for her suffering was his, too.

'Louis…' he said, turning away and dropping his voice as the chef picked up.

'Checking up on me, Jay? I'm in a taxi on my way to the hotel right now.'

'That's brilliant but I'm calling about something else. You mentioned subletting your apartment. Can I take it? Just for a few weeks until your *maman* can find someone long term?'

'You've found your girl?'

'I have, but it's complicated,' he said. 'I'd rather you didn't mention it to anyone.'

'Not even your family?' And when he confirmed that he meant exactly that, Louis said, 'Don't get into any trouble, my friend. Angry husbands are unpredictable.'

'It's not that kind of complicated. It's her family that are the problem.'

'So long as you know what you're doing.'

'Who of us ever knows that?'

Louis laughed. 'Mama will be happy to be spared a trip into Paris in this cold weather. You've stayed before and you know where everything is. There are towels in the airing cupboard, wine in the cooler, the basics in the fridge. You're welcome to whatever you can find. The cleaning service comes early on Saturday and I was saying a fond goodbye to a friend last night, so there are clean sheets on the bed, and everything is dust free.'

'Thanks. Let me know what you need in the way of rent and I'll sort it.'

'No one will be moving in for at least a couple of weeks. Take it with my compliments.' Louis gave him the keycode, then said, 'I appear to

have arrived at the Harrington Park Hotel. It's…
impressive.'

'It was,' Jay said, 'and it will be again with
your help. I owe you, Louis. Call me if you need
anything.'

He ended the call, took a notebook and pen
from his coat pocket and made a note of the keycode, then said, 'It's all fixed.'

'What?'

'I've found somewhere for us to stay while we
sort things out.'

'What things? There's nothing to sort out.
Please, James, don't make this any harder than
it has to be. You've found me and you have your
answers. Go back to London, to your restaurant,
your life.'

'It's not just my life, Chloe. We have a little
girl and I'm going to find her if it's the last thing
I do. For that I need your help.'

'I can't…' She shook her head.

'Can't?' It wasn't this appalling room that was
giving him the shivers. 'Can't or won't?' he demanded.

'Can't. No one can help you find her, James.
It was a closed adoption.'

Closed? The word sounded doom-laden.

'What does that mean?'

'It means that the papers are sealed. I have
no idea who adopted Eloise or where she is. It

will be up to her, once she's eighteen, to choose whether or not to trace me.'

'Not me?'

'Your name isn't on the original birth certificate.' She was struggling to speak, he realised. This was a lot harder for her than she wanted him to see. 'We were not married so you would have had to be there. When she was registered.'

'I'm so sorry,' he said, wanting to hold her, show her how sorry he was, but she was holding herself stiffly, away from him as if afraid that if she let go, she would break… 'I'm so sorry to have to put you through this. To force you to remember.'

'Do you think I could ever forget?' she said fiercely. 'Even for one moment?'

'No. Of course not.'

She reached out and took his hand. 'I'm sorry, James. I'm sorry I wasn't stronger.'

'No,' he said. 'You saved her. Gave her life…'

'And if, some day in the future, she decides to find me, ask me what happened, why I let her go, I'll tell her about a long-ago spring and a lovely boy. A special man… I'll tell her where to find you.' She was smiling through the tears filming her eyes. 'I'll be fine.'

'If you don't die of pneumonia first,' he said, struggling to keep the intense emotion from his voice. 'You really can't stay here, Chloe.'

'James…'

'I'm serious. Can you imagine what the press would do to me if they found out that I'd left the mother of my child living in a freezing room where the walls were running with damp?'

'How would they find out? Any of it?'

'I asked the girl who came to clean my room for your address, Chloe.'

'Oh,' she said. 'That's not good.'

'I was desperate and when she said you were off with the flu, I told her that you'd gone to school with my sister and that Sally would want me to make sure you were okay.'

'And she believed you?'

'Fifty euros dealt with any doubts she might have had.'

'Confirmed them more likely. She'll be telling everyone that I've been flirting with one of the guests.'

'I don't think she recognised me, but it wouldn't take a moment for someone to check who was staying in that room.'

'No matter how careful the management are, there will always be someone who's a stringer for the tabloids. It's just the kind of tip-off they thrive on. Even if it was nothing, they could come up with a headline that would make it seem sordid.'

'And it's not nothing.'

'No.' And it was Chloe's turn to let slip an expletive. 'This is my fault. If I hadn't run away—'

'If it's anyone's fault, it's mine, Chloe. I was so desperate to find you that I didn't think through the consequences. The most incompetent researcher is going to find out that both Sally and I were at St Mary's. A little more digging would turn up the fact that you and I left school midterm in the same week—'

'You were expelled?'

'No.' He shrugged. 'Maybe. I didn't wait to find out. I just wanted to find you.'

'You walked out of school?'

'I knew what I wanted to do,' he said, 'and I didn't need starred A levels or a degree for that.'

She groaned. 'They'll go after Sally, won't they?' Chloe's concern for his sister, so evidently real, warmed him. Gave him hope.

'I'm afraid so. She won't say anything, but they'll have my family history. The hotel is already in the news. And then there's the fact that while your family could give Croesus a run for his money, you are living here.'

'It's not that bad!' she protested.

'Imagine the pictures in the tabloids,' he said. 'They won't focus on the furniture that you've painted, the herbs on the windowsill, the fabrics you've used to make the place more comfortable.'

'Oh, dear Lord…' She looked up at him. 'There will have been gossip at the time and people will swarm out of the woodwork with stories.'

'It's the reality of being in the public eye.'

Her hand tightened around his and for a moment neither of them spoke until the silence was broken by the blasting of a car horn in the street below and a stream of invective from an outraged driver that was clearly audible through the ill-fitting window.

'What are we going to do, James?'

His first instinct had been to go back to London and take Chloe with him. The passion, the desire was as urgent as it had ever been, but they were no longer a couple of teens and the minute he was home, he'd be sucked into pre-Christmas preparations at the restaurant, peace-making between Sally and Hugo, his publication deadline.

She was right. Bad things had happened. They needed time to work through them, to talk, rebuild their relationship.

Right now, nothing was more important than that.

'First things first. You are going to pack— don't leave anything personal behind. Check your rubbish to make sure there's nothing that can lead to you. When you're done, I'll call a taxi and then you are going to disappear.'

'I can't! I have a job!'

'Agency work, you said. Call them and tell them you won't be available until further notice.'

'They'll be annoyed.'

'What can they do? Fire you?'

'But—'

'We are going to the apartment of the chef I've just hired for Harrington's. An informal arrangement with no names on a lease. No paper trail.'

'But…'

'There's a sofa bed in the living room.'

'That's not what's bothering me.' She lifted her shoulders, blushing just a little. 'And my job can be done by anyone, but how can you leave your restaurant?'

'I'm about to give my very talented *sous chef* an early Christmas present by appointing her *chef de cuisine*.'

'But what about your star? Don't they take one away if the *chef de cuisine* leaves?'

'How do you know that?'

'This is France, James. Food is a way of life. I'm right, though.'

He grinned. 'Yes, but I'm not going anywhere. I've been taking on more work, thinking about a second restaurant so I'm less hands-on in the kitchen these days. If I formalise my role to that of executive chef, I think that will cover it. Do you need a hand packing?'

'Um, no… I don't have much,' she said.

She stood up, peeled off his sweater, handed it to him and then stretched up and pulled a holdall from the top shelf of a small wardrobe. She began by lifting the neatly folded contents of her drawers into it. She was right, she didn't have much.

Paris was an expensive place to live, but she was working long hours at two jobs and part time at a third. She should have more than this.

Jay watched her for a moment, the lithe movements of her limbs, the play of light on her skin as she moved to the wardrobe and folded the few garments hanging there and added them to her bag, along with shoe bags, a small box and a folder.

He really hoped she meant it when she said she wasn't bothered about the sofa bed…

She glanced across and caught him staring. 'Can you straighten the bed while I get my stuff from the bathroom?'

'Of course.'

He straightened it out, smoothed the pillows, took the mugs of tea, long gone cold, to the sink and by the time he'd washed them, hung them on their hooks, Chloe had zipped up her bag.

'I'm ready.'

'That's it?'

'Well, the towels and bedlinen are mine. Will we need them?'

She thought she would be coming back here

at some point, he realised, but he didn't want that argument now. He just wanted to get her out of there.

'Not unless there's something special you'll want in the next week or two. Is there anyone you need to tell that you won't be here?' he asked. 'Friends who will worry if you disappear?'

Chloe turned from scanning the flat for anything she might have forgotten and looked at him.

'A man, you mean?'

Of course a man. Chloe was a lovely young woman. It was inconceivable that she hadn't been involved with anyone in all this time.

'The woman at the hotel knows where you live,' he said quickly. 'I thought she might be a friend.'

'A friend wouldn't have handed over my address for fifty euros. Not without asking me first,' she pointed out, then gave a little sigh. 'One of the women at the hotel was looking for somewhere to live. There was a studio vacant on the second floor, so I wrote down the address and the number of the landlord. She was already fixed up, but she pinned it to the noticeboard in case anyone else needed a place. Anyone could have seen it.'

'What about neighbours?'

'We're all out at work. I rarely see anyone. Shall we go?' she said, reaching for her coat. 'No need to call a taxi. It'll be quicker on the Metro.' She wound a scarf around her neck. 'And that won't leave a trail.'

'Am I being paranoid?' he asked.

'Probably,' she said, 'but we've been hiding our relationship since we spent the entire end-of-term Christmas disco at opposite ends of the hall trying not to look at one another. Why change things now?'

'You danced with George McKinnon.'

'Poor George. You took him down in the rugby match the next day.'

'It's all part of the game.'

'You were on the same team! And you danced all evening, too. I didn't lose it when Lydia Grafton produced a piece of mistletoe and kissed you.'

'Why not?' he asked, reaching for his coat, buttoning it.

'I felt sorry for her.' She lifted her shoulders in an awkward little shrug, clearly wishing she hadn't got into this. 'You were top of her Christmas list, James, but I knew that Santa wasn't going to deliver. You'd already given yourself to me.'

'*Plus ça change, plus c'est même chose*, Chloe,' he said, shouldering his backpack and picking up her bag.

Plus ça change…

CHAPTER FIVE

'THIS IS A lovely apartment...'

Jay followed Chloe as she explored her new surroundings, running her fingers along the arm of a soft leather sofa. Glancing out of the tall windows to the street below.

The apartment was one floor above a pretty courtyard in the Latin Quarter, with its Left Bank vibe, and he could well understand why his friend would want to hang onto it, no matter where in the world he was based.

She opened the door to the bedroom and paused, just for a moment, before glancing back at him. 'What was that you said about a bigger bed?'

It wasn't just bigger, it was enormous.

'Chloe, what happened...the sex...' He raked a hand through his hair, a nervous gesture he'd long grown out of. 'It wasn't... I didn't mean to...'

'I was there, James. It happened to both of us,' she said, when he stumbled to a halt. 'It always did.'

'Yes…' His throat was so dry he could hardly speak. 'But I just wanted to make it clear that whatever happens is your decision. This is your place, your rules. I've slept on the sofa before.'

She nodded, giving him no clue to her thoughts, and when she went to check out the bathroom he didn't follow. He'd stayed with Louis one New Year and he knew that it had a roomy walk-in shower and a tub large enough for two. He didn't need that image in his head right now.

'Are you hungry?' he asked, when she'd explored the bathroom and was fidgeting around the apartment. Looking but not looking.

'To be honest I don't know what I am. Everything happened so fast. You've yanked me out of my home, my job, my world,' she said, with a gesture that took in her surroundings, but not owning them. 'I understand why, but what happens next? How am I going to live, James? What am I going to do?'

Her words brought him up short. Even without the possibility of paparazzi interest, getting her out of that ghastly room had been the right thing to do, but he'd turned up out of the blue, taken over her life and the sex had seriously complicated things.

He'd backed off pushing the physical side of their relationship, but he hadn't given much thought to the future beyond getting her back to London and into his life.

He wanted to take her hand, hold her, reassure her that it was all going to be okay, but she'd suffered in ways he couldn't begin to imagine and it was clear that she needed some time, space to make sense of everything that had happened.

Maybe they both did.

'When was the last time you had a holiday?' he asked.

'I, um… I haven't…' He waited. 'If you mean a real holiday, then it was the week we spent at the cottage.'

'That makes two of us,' he said. 'Maybe this is the moment for us both to take time out of our real worlds and have some fun. Leave the future to take care of itself for a couple of weeks?'

'Fun?'

'That wasn't a euphemism for sex, Chloe. I was thinking that we could take a ride up the Eiffel Tower, have dinner on a Bateau Mouche, take a trip on a tour bus.' They were the first things that came to mind but there had to be a lot more. 'All those things that you don't bother to do when you live in Paris because they're always there.'

'It's not exactly the weather for a ride on an open-topped bus.'

She was still struggling, but she hadn't responded with a flat-out no.

'We'll just have to wrap up warm and take a flask of coffee laced with brandy.'

Even as he said it, he was remembering a freezing night when they'd thawed out in a warm, candlelit bath and, as their eyes met, a flush of pink stained her cheeks and he knew she was remembering it, too.

'We can queue for bread straight from the oven,' he said, seizing the moment. 'Shop in the markets like real Parisiens and pay a visit to Dehillerin. I need new copper pans for the restaurant, and you can help me choose.'

'Not all fun, then?' Chloe said, shaking her head, but she was smiling now.

'When you're a kid you take your pocket money to Hamleys in Regent Street,' he said. 'When you're a chef, you take it to the Paris emporium founded by Eugene de Hillerin a century ago. It will make a great blog post.'

'I'm sure it will,' she said, 'but if that backpack contains everything that you brought with you, I think your first stop had better be for some spare clothes.'

He groaned. 'I hate shopping for clothes.'

She rolled her eyes at him. 'Do you want me to come and hold your hand?' she asked, and he felt the tension seep out of him.

'I'll treat you to breakfast at Café de Flore before we face the ordeal,' he said. 'Why don't you unpack and think about what else you'd like to do while I make a couple of calls and then we'll find somewhere interesting to eat?'

'James…' He waited, but she shook her head. 'Nothing.'

Chloe left James to his phone calls. She didn't have much to unpack and once that was done, she lay back on the gorgeous bed, stretching out limbs heavy with the delicious lassitude that followed vigorous sex.

It felt like coming alive after a long dark winter.

Her Sleeping Beauty moment…

She groaned at the cliché of James climbing the castle wall to wake her with a kiss. It suggested that she had been a passive recipient, when in reality it had been a wholly mutual body slam and one that her body, so long deprived, was eager to repeat.

Her brain, on the other hand, was sending out confused messages.

Its pleasure centre had been jolted out of stasis. Long undisturbed parts of her body were throbbing out a demand for more while health and safety central, the area that had guided every step since she'd chosen freedom over comfort, was frantically flashing a red light.

A warning that this could only end in tears.

James, certain that they could pick up where they left off and carry on as if nothing had happened, reminded her so much of the boy she'd fallen in love with. Eager, full of plans and, when she'd told him that she was pregnant, so sure of their future together as a family. He'd brushed aside her anxieties, ready to confront her parents and, despite his youth, be a man.

And he had been all of that.

He'd been strong, fought tooth and nail to find her and when his efforts had been blocked by lawyers, he hadn't crawled away into a hole. He'd had no family to support him, but he'd done all the things he'd talked about and made a success of his life.

She was the one who'd been weak, crumbled under pressure.

Maybe this would all end in tears but, with James or without him, this was a wake-up call.

It was time to stop running and take hold of her life. Remember her dreams.

Jay chose a bottle of a fine Pouilly-Fuissé from the wine chiller, opened it, poured two glasses and then settled down on the sofa to call Sally and let her know what had happened.

When it went straight to voicemail, and he realised that with the seven-hour time difference it would be close to three a.m. in the Far East, he didn't bother to leave a message, and instead called Freya, his talented *sous chef.*

'Chef?'

'Freya, a personal matter has come up here in Paris. I'll have to stay on for a while.'

'We will manage, chef.'

'I know you will,' he said, 'which is why I'm appointing you *chef de cuisine* at L'Étranger.'

'As a temporary measure?'

Freya was the epitome of Scandi cool, but she hadn't been able to contain the audible gulp before she asked the question.

'No, not temporary. We both know that I've been doing less hands-on work in the kitchen in recent months. With so many new projects demanding my attention that isn't going to change so it makes sense for me to move to the role of executive chef. We'll discuss the financial implications and any changes you might want to make to the menu when I return. You can call me at any time.'

'Yes, chef. Thank you, chef.' She cleared her throat. 'Jay?'

'Freya?'

'Is everything okay?'

He smiled at her unexpected concern. 'Everything' was a long way from certain, but then Chloe appeared in the doorway, causing the same life-changing hitch in his breath that he'd experienced the very first time he'd noticed her, and he said, 'Yes, chef.'

He disconnected, tossed the phone on the table.

A simple little black dress clung to her body; her fair curls had been brushed out around her shoulders. Just looking at her gave him goose bumps but, unlike earlier, when they'd been wordlessly drawn to one another, the silence felt like a force field that was holding them apart.

'Are you finished with your calls?' she asked, when the silence had gone on for far too long.

'Yes… I'd hoped to speak to Sally. She'll want to know that I found you,' he said, rushing on to fill the void, 'but I forgot about the time difference.'

'Time difference? Where is she?'

'Singapore. A lot has happened in the last few weeks. It's why I'm in Paris. But I've sorted out things at the restaurant. No one is expecting me back…' He took a breath, picked up the glasses and handed her one. 'You look…very French.'

'Do I?' She smoothed the cloth across her stomach in a self-conscious gesture. 'French-women buy classic, keep their clothes for a long time and have no hang-ups about being seen wearing the same thing many times. So well spotted.'

'I'm not sure if I've paid you a compliment or not,' he said uncertainly. Chloe didn't help him out and he struggled on. 'If you have a dress you love, that looks fabulous on you, why wouldn't you want to wear it more than once?'

'It beats me,' she said, clinking her glass against his, 'but I'll drink to fabulous.' They both took a mouthful of the very fine wine. 'And fun.'

Something had changed while he was talking to Freya.

Chloe had been through horrors he could not begin to imagine and today she had not only relived that nightmare for him, but once again, because of him, she had been forced to leave everything she knew.

He'd spent years planning what he'd say if he ever saw her again, but at that moment the words were all wrong, overblown, ridiculous…

'To fun,' he repeated.

They just stood for a long moment, looking at one another until he drained his glass and said, 'Drink up. We need to get out of here.'

James took her arm as they wandered through streets thronged with tourists seeking out the Left Bank vibe, the haunts of writers such as Hemingway and Sartre.

The evening was cold, but the air was filled with the rich spicy scent of food from all parts of the world. Couples were clinging to each other, and not just the young. Stores were lit up with Christmas lights and it should have been magical, but it wasn't and Chloe dug the heels of her boots into the pavement, bringing them to a halt.

'Pardon,' he said, apologising to people behind them who were forced to swerve around them and didn't hesitate to voice their feelings. 'Are you okay, Chloe?'

'No,' she said, pulling her arm free. 'This isn't going to work.'

'I don't understand.'

She raised an eyebrow. 'Really? We know one another more intimately than anyone else on earth and yet you're holding my arm as gingerly as if I was an elderly great-aunt with an uncertain temper. One who will lash out with her stick if you get too close.'

He laughed, but without conviction.

'Don't!' she said, and he lifted a hand in silent apology. 'If you feel awkward, I can handle it, but you don't have to pretend just because we had sex.'

A couple of passers-by whistled, and James looked around a little desperately. 'Could you lower your voice just a little?'

'I've had more contact with a stranger on the

Metro,' she hissed and walked on, forcing him to follow her. 'Because that's what you are. It's above the door of your restaurant. L'Étranger. Which is weird, by the way. You don't eat with strangers.'

'It doesn't just mean "stranger",' he said. 'It also means "outsider".'

Outsider? 'Is that how you see yourself?' she asked, shocked.

'It's how everyone else saw me when I came to work in Paris. I'd lost pretty much everyone, everything I was ever close to. My parents, Hugo, my home, you and our baby. It was a recurring theme and I was done with it. If I didn't get close to anyone, I couldn't lose them.'

'Oh, James. I'm sorry. That's such a dark place...' Aware that he was looking at her, she said, 'My breakdown was postnatal depression brought on by grief.'

'Your father should be horsewhipped.'

'And what would that achieve? The damage is done.' She shook her head. 'I had nothing, James, but you were able to focus all those feelings, all your heart, on your career. On the dishes you create.'

'Assemble the best ingredients, treat them with respect and they will always deliver.'

Unlike people. He didn't say it. He didn't need to.

For a moment they just looked at one another as people swerved around them, then she took his arm, tucked it firmly beneath hers and said, 'Come on. Enough with the navel-gazing. Let's eat.'

There were no shortages of places to choose from, but James led the way down a narrow alleyway to a small restaurant. It was busy but when he told the *maître d'* that it had been recommended by Louis Joubert, they were immediately shown to a table by the window.

'What would you like to drink?'

'I'm regretting the expensive glass of wine I didn't finish when you rushed me out of the flat,' she said, smiling at the waiter as he handed her a menu.

'Blame our hasty exit on your dress.'

'Really?' She turned to look at him. 'If I'd known that was the problem, I'd have taken it off.'

'Chloe…'

'I dreamed about this, James. How, one day, you would walk back into my life.'

'Oh? How did it go?'

'The usual way. Like one of those perfect, soft-focus movie moments. The last scene of *Sleepless in Seattle*…'

He looked baffled. 'I don't know that movie.'

She rolled her eyes. 'It does lack a woman-eating shark…' She shook her head. 'It doesn't matter. It was never going to happen, not like that.'

'But we did meet.'

'Yes, but it was more like one of those dreams where you're caught naked in public.'

He frowned. 'You ran away because you were embarrassed because you were working as a maid?'

'About as embarrassed as you'd have been if I'd seen you taking out the rubbish in a burger joint,' she said, but it had been more than that. She'd run from the uncertainty, the fear of rejection… 'Be honest, James, what did you think?'

'Think? I don't know. I was too shocked for anything coherent…'

'That's reality for you. Real life isn't a soft-focus dream and sometimes, no matter how great the ingredients, the sauce curdles.'

'I came after you,' he protested. 'I was half-way down the back stairs when I realised how it would look if I burst into the staffroom in pursuit of a maid.' He sighed. 'I was thinking too much by then. I should have just kept going and to hell with what anyone thought.'

'You wouldn't have found me. I was out of the door and gone.'

'I did find something.' He went to his coat and

returned with something that gleamed silver in the candlelight.

Chloe gave a little gasp as she recognised the distorted Celtic swirl of the hair pin James had bought her for her seventeenth birthday.

'It my hairpin,' she said, automatically lifting her hand to where it would normally be tucked into the bun she wore when she was working.

'You must have lost it in your haste and I'm afraid I crushed it as I pounded down the stairs after you.'

'I shouldn't have worn something so precious to work, but some days I needed it.'

She reached out to take it, but he returned it to his pocket.

'I'll have it fixed.'

'It will cost more than it's worth.'

'The fact that it's precious to you, that you wanted to wear it, makes it worth any amount of money to restore it.'

She had to swallow hard to shift the lump in her throat before she could thank him.

'You weren't the only one who dreamed, Chloe. I dreamed, too.'

'In soft focus?'

He shook his head. 'I dreamed about what I would say to you.'

'Hello was a good start.'

'It went downhill from there.'

'It was a bit of a bumpy ride,' she agreed, 'but there were some good bits.'

'Well, that's encouraging. Are you going to give me a clue?'

'I think we need to decide what we're going to eat,' she said, turning to the menu. 'Now, are you going to get all cheffy and insist on talking me through it, or can I just go ahead and order the butternut squash soup and the tagine?'

He ordered the soup for both of them, the tagine for Chloe and fish skewers with ginger served with a risotto for himself and took the waiter's recommendation for a wine robust enough to cope with the spices.

'Your French is very good, James. How did you end up working in Paris?'

'Someone I worked for in the school holidays, an old friend of my father, gave me a job after I walked out of school and, later, he organised a placement for me at one of the big Paris hotels. It's where I met Louis Joubert, the man whose apartment we're camping in.'

'Where is he? Louis?'

'He's in London. At the Harrington Park Hotel. Nick Wolfe finally drove it to bankruptcy. Sally and I were going to make an offer to the creditors, but before we could get all the finances in place it was bought from under us. By Hugo.'

'Hugo?' She thought for a moment. 'Your

older brother who disappeared?' James hadn't talked about his brother at school. As far as anyone there knew, he and Sally had no other family. But he'd opened his heart to her... 'He's back?'

'We had a message that the new owner wanted to talk to the Harrington twins. We thought that maybe they wanted to involve us in some way, make capital out of the family connection, but when we walked into the lawyer's office Hugo was waiting for us.'

'That's incredible!' She sat back in her chair. 'That must have been such a shock. Like seeing a ghost.'

'Apparently it's the season for it.'

She waved that away. 'Where has he been all this time?'

Over the food he told her Hugo's story, his plans to restore the hotel, his desire to involve them both.

'That's...' She shook her head because there were no words. 'You must be overjoyed to have him back.'

'I... Yes. After the initial shock. When I'd heard his story. Sally is finding it harder. She can't get her head around why he stayed away for so long. Why he never sent so much as a postcard. He didn't even know, until he got to London, that our mother had been killed in a car accident.'

She swallowed. She didn't have to imagine how it felt to have someone disappear from your life. To have no idea where they were or if they were alive.

She knew.

'Do you understand?' she asked.

He nodded. 'Mum turned her back on him. That's hard to forgive but she was vulnerable, and Nick Wolfe was an accomplished manipulator...'

'Poor Hugo. Poor Sally.'

'She's struggling to forgive him, but she'll get there. She has agreed to handle the design brief for the hotel, which is a start.'

'And you came to Paris to find Hugo a chef?'

'Job done. I already had Louis at the top of the list I'd drawn up in the event that we managed to get the hotel ourselves. I thought it would be a tough sell, but Louis was ripe for a move.'

'And now you've found me. Your list of the lost is getting shorter. And the hotel, your home, is back in your family.'

He nodded, but his mouth tightened, and she knew that he was thinking of their daughter.

She put her hand over his. 'How many years was Hugo lost to you, James? How many years since we were together?'

'Too long,' he said.

'But we endured the dark times,' she said. 'We

survived, carried on living and Eloise will be eighteen in just over eight years. If she needs us, she will find us.'

His hand turned and he grasped hers. 'And if she doesn't?'

He sounded despairing but she had lived with that thought a long time and had an answer.

'We will know that she doesn't need us, James. That she's happy, with a family who love her.'

CHAPTER SIX

JAMES NODDED HIS acceptance of what she'd said and, as the waiter arrived with their food, released her hand and sat back.

The soup was rich, unctuous, warming with a hint of fish stock and a cluster of large prawns.

'That has to be the best thing I've eaten in for ever,' she said. 'Was there some chilli in there? I feel warmed to my boots.'

'Just enough for a little heat, not enough to get in the way of the flavour. Perfectly balanced.'

Food took them away from the fraught discussion of the past. James told her about the places he'd worked, some good, some ghastly. About the television show that had given him his big break. About the ups and downs of starting his own restaurant.

They were finally able to relax, laugh and when, a couple of hours later, they walked back out into the street, James took her hand as if it was the most natural thing in the world.

'Thank you, James. It's a long time since I ate in a good restaurant.'

'Food is one of the most important constituents of a holiday. Besides, I don't often have the chance to do this. It's important to get out there, see what good food is on offer.'

'A bit of a busman's holiday, then. Can a chef ever just enjoy a meal without analysing it?' she asked.

'Identifying some subtle ingredient is half the fun, but it's possible. Can you ever look at a bed without wanting to straighten the corners?' he asked.

He was grinning and she laughed as she shook her head, said, 'Thanks for reminding me about the day job. You are going to have to cheer me up by describing the best dish you've ever tasted.'

'Oh, that's a tough one...'

She suggested a few classics, but he shook his head. 'I've tasted some of the greatest dishes, prepared by world-famous chefs,' he said, 'but the magic comes from more than what's on the plate in front of you.'

'Don't tell the food bloggers that!'

'Believe me, I'm not going to discourage them,' he assured her. 'They're good for business and a restaurant dish has to have eye appeal as well as the perfect blend of flavours.'

'But?' She glanced at him. 'There was definitely a lingering "but" hanging around the end of that sentence.'

He pulled her hand beneath his arm, drawing her close. 'The temperature has dropped like a stone. Add hats and gloves to the shopping list,' he said.

'Hats and gloves,' she repeated. 'But?'

He paused at a crossing, watching the traffic, waiting for it to come to a halt before they could cross the road. For a moment she thought he wasn't going to respond to the prompt, and she left it as they turned the corner in the courtyard, but as he punched in the keycode, he said, 'You're right about the "but". Eating is about more than a pretty dish. It's an emotional experience.'

'So not what I expected.'

'It's not about how trendy the restaurant is, or the number of Michelin stars it can boast,' he said. 'It's who you're with that makes food memorable.'

He opened the door, stood back to let her lead the way.

Inside, the flat was warm, and he shed his coat, not looking at her, because it wasn't some dish he was remembering, she realised. It was about who he'd been with when he ate it. Someone else...

She took a breath, wishing she'd never gone down this path, but knowing that she couldn't stop. 'Are you going to tell me?'

'If I tell you,' he said, turning to look at her,

his face expressionless, 'my reputation will be entirely in your hands.'

For a moment she was taken in, then she cuffed his arm as she realised that he was teasing. 'You still do that!'

'And you still fall for it.'

She unbuttoned her coat, and he took it from her, giving her a moment to catch her breath while he hung it with his in the lobby. Loving that he was still, deep down, the boy she'd fallen in love with. Afraid of the rush of pleasure it gave her.

'Tea, coffee?' he asked, picking up the wine glasses as he headed for the kitchen.

'There's tea?'

'Herbal stuff. Camomile, spiced ginger, mint? We'll go to Galeries Lafayette and pick up the real thing in the morning. Or there's chocolate?'

'No, I'm fine.'

She could hear him moving about in the kitchen, water running as he washed the glasses. 'Have you guessed yet?' he called after a few moments.

She sank into the soft leather of the sofa, stretched out her legs and cast her mind back.

'It has to be comfort food of some kind?' He didn't answer and she tried to think of the best/worst comfort food she knew. 'A chip butty?'

'Are you referring to the perfection that is a

soft bap, split open, filled with chunky fries and covered with curry sauce?'

'That was the rugby-team version. I prefer mine dipped in mayonnaise.'

'You don't know what you're missing,' he said. 'Try again.'

The kitchen on their floor at school had been equipped with a toaster but it had so much use that it was always breaking down, so James had brought in his own and kept it in his room. And a camping gas ring that broke every rule.

She remembered toasted muffins with raspberry jam that tasted of summer. He'd had the biggest pot of Marmite you could buy and on cold winter nights he would heat up tomato soup out of a tin…

When she looked up, he was leaning against the door, watching her, waiting for the penny to drop. And finally, it did.

It was not something they'd eaten at school but late one night in the little cottage by the sea and her heart turned over at the memory of that day, that moment…

'It's a fried-egg sandwich.' Before she could draw one shaky breath, he was beside her, taking her hand. She laughed a little shakily and said, 'But not just any fried-egg sandwich.'

'The eggs have to be free range,' he said,

'bought at the farm gate. They have to be fried in butter...'

They were so close that she could feel his breath on her ear, her cheek...

'...and generously dolloped with brown sauce, squished between slices of thick white bread. And the yolk has to be runny enough to spill out over your fingers when you bite into it.'

The image was so real that she could almost feel the yolk, taste the sharpness of the sauce...

'Licking your fingers is half the fun,' she said.

'Licking someone else's is the other half...'

'It was the last Friday in May,' she said, because someone should keep talking or they were going to do something stupid and she was so determined not to do that stupid thing...

'We'd been on the beach hunting for fossils.'

The sun had been shining, but the sky was streaked with mare's tails from a storm that had passed in the night. And right now, her heart was pounding, her lips burning...

'You found an ammonite.'

'A big one. I don't know what happened to it.'

'You left it in my room. I still have it. That, and a book of poetry that you gave me, the photographs of you on my phone and the clothes I stood up in, were all I took away from school.'

She turned to look at him. 'Sonnets from the Portuguese. "I thought once how Theocritus had sung… Of the sweet years, the dear and wished for years…"'

For a long moment they looked at one another and then James said, 'We had to leave the next morning and you insisted on going for a swim even though the water was freezing. Afterwards you were shivering so much that I ran you a bath so that you could warm up…'

'My fingers were so cold I couldn't manage the buttons. You did them up all wrong,' she said.

He grinned. 'I undid them all right.'

'You were always good at that part.'

'You had sand in your hair, sticking to your skin…'

'I was cold and sore where it had rubbed.' The breath was being squeezed out of her body and the touch of her clothes against her skin was torture.

'Sand gets everywhere.'

His breath was on her lips, warming her as he had that day, his soapy hands sliding over her breasts, her thighs, between her toes—any place where a grain of sand might cling…

Did her lips touch his first or did he move to close the space between them? It didn't matter. All that mattered was that they were together, that she was melting into a kiss so sweet, so mesmerisingly slow that she barely noticed the moment that she opened her mouth to the sensuously sweet dance of his tongue.

This was her soft-focus dream moment and she drew back just long enough to say, 'The sandwich was epic, James, but let's skip it and go straight to the bath.'

Chloe stirred, stretched.

Jay had been watching her for a while, completely blown away by the unexpected way she had opened up to him last night, become again the seventeen-year-old girl who had thrown away every last vestige of reserve.

Wondering if she would be happy about it in the cold light of day.

She'd been up and down, all evening. Flirty and distant in turn. He'd understood. She'd been through so much and talking to him had clearly brought back painful memories.

Despite that first explosive moment, he'd had no intention of pushing her into an intimate relationship. He'd waited years for this and wasn't about to ruin things by pushing her into something she'd regret.

In the end he hadn't had to push. All it had taken was a throwaway remark, to spark the memory of a special moment when they'd been happy, for her to fall, taking him with her.

The cottage had given them so much freedom. They hadn't had to hide their feelings from disapproving teachers, gossipy girls.

They'd held hands as they'd walked to the beach, laughed a lot, done their bit to save water by sharing showers, been as noisy as they liked when they'd made love.

But that day had been different. What had started as a problem with buttons had built into a no-holds-barred, sensually devastating experience in which Chloe had given everything, demanded everything, with consequences that had changed both their lives. Hers, far more than his.

He bent and gently kissed her lovely mouth. 'Wake up, sleeping beauty.'

'I'm not asleep.' She opened her eyes and what he was seeing was not regret.

'I've been lying here afraid that I was dreaming and that if I opened my eyes, this would all vanish and I'd have to dash to my freezing bathroom, cram into the Metro and spend the entire day making beds and cleaning hotel rooms.'

'It's not going to happen. You're on holiday and so am I.'

'We're on holiday and we're lying in bed wasting the day?'

'Who said anything about wasting it?' Confident now, he propped himself up on his elbow, ran the back of a finger along the curve of her shoulder. 'You look positively edible lying on that pillow.'

'Edible?' She raised an eyebrow. 'Is that what chefs say to a woman when they want to—?'

He put a finger to her lips.

'You are the only woman I've ever said it to, Chloe. I've been too busy building a career, building a business, to waste time indulging in casual sex.'

'Why would it be casual?' She frowned. 'There was no one?'

'There was always someone, Chloe. Just because she wasn't there, I couldn't see her, touch her, didn't change that.'

Lost for words as she took in the enormity of what he'd just said, she reached up, took his face between her hands and said, 'Ditto.'

'That's from one of your movies. There was a song you loved…' But she was kissing him, and he lost the thread.

They shopped in designer outlets in the Marais district. James topped up his wardrobe, bought a scarf. Chloe tried on a bright red coat. She needed a new coat and she was tired of wearing black.

James wanted to buy it for her, but although she wasn't working, she insisted on paying for it herself. She thought he was going to argue, but maybe something in her stance warned him not to push it. Instead he bought her a white faux-fur hat.

'I look ridiculous,' she said. 'And I never wear hats.'

'You look gorgeous and you're going to need it when we go on the bus tour.'

They ate *soupe du jour* in a bistro, which turned out to be leek and potato, but nothing like the way they had made it at school. Afterwards, while they had coffee, James checked his phone.

'Problems?' she asked, when he'd been busy on it for a few minutes.

He looked up. 'Sorry… I didn't mean to ignore you.'

'It's okay. You must have stuff that needs your attention.'

'I do, but my attention was totally focussed on booking dinner on a Bateau Mouche for this evening.'

'Oh.'

'Was that a happy "oh"? Or a *That is such a tourist thing to do* "oh"?'

It had been a surprised, *It would have been nice to talk about it or to have been asked first* 'oh', but he had wanted to give her a treat so she said, 'You did say we were going to behave like total tourists so it was a surprised, happy, *How lovely! I've lived in Paris for years and never done that* "oh".'

He grinned. 'I can't believe the things I never did when I was living here. I haven't even seen the Mona Lisa.'

'I am shocked.'

'You go to see her regularly, I assume.'

'Every week and twice on Sundays.' Then, grinning, she shook her head. 'It's been a while,' she admitted. 'It takes more than a moody portrait to impress a teenage girl.'

'A moody portrait?' He shook his head in disbelief. 'What about the enigmatic smile that everyone raves about?'

'If you must know, I gave her four out of ten for effort. I swear that if she'd been wearing a watch, she'd have been sneaking a glance and wondering how much longer Leonardo was going to take.'

He laughed. 'That's harsh.'

'Maybe I was projecting my own feelings onto her,' she admitted. 'The adults were droning on endlessly about the pictures, the sculptures and a ceiling that they stared at for what seemed like hours.'

'You really didn't have a good time.'

'You want the truth?'

'Will I be able to handle it?'

'I was thirteen. It was Paris Fashion Week and instead of having a sneaky sip of champagne at Dior with my mother, my father insisted that I accompany him on a tour of the Louvre.'

'A sulky teenager? I'll bet he regretted that.'

She sighed. 'I knew better than to show my feelings. I was very polite to the *directeur* and his guests, smiled in all the appropriate places, even asked a question or two. I knew how to make Papa proud.' She shrugged. 'Until I didn't.'

'I'm so sorry, Chloe.'

She reached out, took his hand. 'Don't be, James. Don't ever be sorry. I've never, for one moment, regretted what happened between us.'

'Ditto…' He drew back, aware that wasn't an appropriate response but couldn't have said why. 'But let's give the Louvre a miss.' He called for the bill, then said, 'It's not fashion week, but we could find a Dior boutique?'

She shook her head, touched that he would be so thoughtful. 'We're doing the tourist trail, it's on every sightseer's bucket list and it's long past time that I gave the old girl another chance.'

They took their purchases back to the flat, Chloe changed into her new coat and they caught the bus from the Sorbonne to the Pont des Arts and walked across the bridge.

'This isn't good. I should have booked a skip-the-queue ticket,' James said as he saw the mass of people waiting to clear security.

'No need.' Chloe tugged him away. 'We'll go in through the Carrousel du Louvre.'

She led the way through the underground shopping precinct, followed the signs and ten minutes later they were inside the museum.

'The Mona Lisa is in Italian Renaissance next

to the Salle Denon, but there is a lot of other really fabulous stuff you have to see.'

He'd been downloading the museum app to his phone, but now he looked up, clearly surprised that she'd remembered. 'How long ago did you say you were here?'

'My father was a patron.' She gave an awkward little shrug. 'He probably still is... He considered the appreciation of fine art to be preparation for the life I would live. There was more than one private visit.'

He frowned. 'I didn't have the slightest clue just how different your life was from the rest of us, did I?'

'No,' she said, putting an arm through his to hold him close, 'but that means it's your lucky day. I have a retentive memory so forget the app. You are about to get the advantage of my privileged lifestyle for the price of two tickets.'

He didn't move, just looked at her.

'It's a bargain,' she prompted.

He took a breath. 'Yes, sorry... Where do we start?'

'With Canova's Psyche and Cupid.'

They stood in front of the exquisite marble sculpture while Chloe gave him a potted history of Canova and its subject. 'Their story is one of forbidden love and, after many trials, redemption.'

'Is redemption the same as happy ever after?' he asked,

'Well, it's a Greek myth, so it's not quite that simple.'

He turned from the sculpture to look at her. 'Like life, then.'

She nodded. 'Just like life.'

'That was incredible,' Jay said, a couple of hours later, as they walked through the Christmas fair in the Tuileries, looking at the craft stalls.

'I have to admit that it was a lot more fun with you than my father.'

'I'm relieved to hear it. And fun is what we're about.'

He bought mulled wine and then stopped to look at some hand-blown glass Christmas ornaments. 'As children, we all used to choose a new ornament each year and hang it on the tree set up in the reception area of the Harrington Park,' he said.

'You're not children any more,' she said. 'And Hugo might not want a tree with all those memories attached to it.'

'We're all children at Christmas,' he said. 'And the tree is part of Harrington history. Which would you choose?'

He watched as Chloe looked at the ornaments, occasionally picking one up. 'The glass bell is very pretty…'

'But?'

'A bit safe. If it were up to me, I'd choose the flamingo.'

'The flamingo it is. And I'll take Cupid.' He nodded to the stallholder. 'It will remind me of our visit to the Louvre.' And because Chloe would be there to hang her own ornament on the tree. 'You weren't kidding about your memory, were you? By the time we reached that ceiling—which was truly amazing, by the way—you had quite an audience. Several people asked if they could book you for a private tour.'

'What a pity I didn't have a card for you to hand out. I could set up my own private tour service.'

He paused at a stall selling cheese to cover his shock at what she'd just said. 'Why would you want to be a tour guide?'

'The tips are good.'

Not going to happen. This was a pause, a little time out, while they reconnected. After an uncertain start, it had been going so well and it was just a matter of time before she returned to London with him and they restarted the clock on their lives.

He'd handed over the kitchen to Freya, and he could write anywhere, but he had other commitments. An awards dinner where he was booked to present one of the prizes. Meetings that couldn't be cancelled…

'I'm sure they are,' he said, 'but do you think your life would be better with four jobs?'

He accepted a sliver of sheep's cheese from the stallholder. It might as well have been cardboard.

'I could give up the cleaning,' she said, oblivious to the edge in his voice, or deliberately ignoring it as she tried a blue-veined cheese. 'Oh, I like that…' She held out a taster for him to try. 'It's really good, James. Creamy, salty…'

He took it, tasted nothing, but she was waiting for a reaction. 'Yes, it's very good.'

Maybe he lacked conviction, because she sighed and finally stopped avoiding his question.

'I may have rejected my family, James, but the spirit of entrepreneurship is imprinted in the Forbes Scott genes. It's why I work three jobs and save every cent so that when the right moment comes, I'll be ready.'

He frowned. Ready for what?

'This is your moment, Chloe. There's going to be a book in the spring, more television and I'm in talks with a major hotel about establishing an on-site afternoon-tea service. L'Étranger is going to be a brand. I want you to be a part of that.'

He'd hoped to impress her with his own drive, anticipated some enthusiasm, but she frowned. 'Won't Hugo be offended if you go to a rival?'

Hugo? He shook his head. 'I've already talked to him. He's fine about it.'

'Are you sure?'

She turned to the stallholder to ask him for a hundred and fifty grams of the blue cheese and the only thing he was sure about was that she hadn't responded to his expectation that she would return to London with him. To working with him. Being with him.

'It's possible that he's accepted your decision because he wants to keep you happy,' she said.

'Hugo and I are fine.' She raised an eyebrow. 'We are,' he insisted.

'I hope you're right, but the fracture in your family is complicated. You were split apart by the appalling deceit of one man and, despite the fact that you were children, it's inevitable that you will feel guilt for not having seen the truth.'

What?

'That's crazy,' he protested.

She didn't argue. 'Isn't that why Sally is so angry with him? The reason you are keeping him at a distance?'

'No! I'm not…' The objection was automatic, too quick, and he pulled a face. 'I don't know.'

'You're both afraid that Hugo will disappear again. That's a perfectly natural response, James, and your brother clearly understands that it's going to take time to build trust and knit your family back together. He's not going to do anything to jeopardise that.'

'Is that how it is with us, Chloe?' he asked.

'You never knew why Hugo disappeared, James. That's like a death, but without a body to grieve over.' She took the cheese, paid for it while he was still trying to get his head around that. 'It was different for us. We both knew what had happened, why it happened. Our tragedy was that there was nothing we could do about it.'

'But it doesn't have to end there. Cupid and Psyche had their lives messed up by family—'

'My father is a powerful man, James. He is not a god,' she said, handing him the little paper carrier. 'This is for you. Cheese is very good for the bones.'

But whose bones? Unsure of the answer, he was disinclined to ask. But he would call Hugo later and talk to him. Really talk to him. Ask him how things were going, tell him about Chloe. Maybe broach the question of the afternoon-tea service again, but right now he didn't want to think about any of that.

'Cheese is one of life's great joys,' he said, 'but right now you have to make a really big decision.'

'James…'

'Are we going to take a ride on the Ferris wheel, or risk our bones on the ice rink?'

CHAPTER SEVEN

'Don't!' Chloe shook her head as Jay held up his phone to take a video of her with the Eiffel Tower flashing behind her. 'Could you behave any more like a tourist?' she hissed.

'No one but a tourist would be coming on this cruise. Look around you, everyone is doing the same thing. I'm just going to send this to Sally and Hugo so that they can see that we're having a good time.'

He'd called Hugo while Chloe had gone out to buy a new lipstick, and over a long conversation had told him what had happened in the past. Why he was staying in Paris.

Hugo had asked one or two questions, but mostly he'd just listened.

For now, Jay was doing his best to forget about the things that were piling up in London, steering clear of the future and concentrating on the moment.

Chloe rolled her eyes, shook her head, but gave a little wave and said, '*Bonjour*, Sally! *Bonjour*, Hugo!'

He clicked away for a moment and then said, 'All done. The modern equivalent of the postcard.'

The boat began to pull away from the dock, the waitress topped up their glasses, they smiled for the boat's photographer when she stopped at their table.

Food arrived, scallops, duck, something frivolous in chocolate, all delicious but it wasn't about the food. It was about watching Chloe's reflection in the glass canopy as she gazed out at the river. About being with her.

She looked pensive, faraway and he suspected that she wasn't seeing the passing boats, the impressive floodlit buildings, the Ferris wheel from which they'd seen Paris lighting up beneath their feet earlier that evening.

She turned and saw him watching her. 'You're not looking.'

'Yes, I am,' he said. 'I'm looking and looking.'

She blushed, smiled. 'This is lovely. Thank you, James.'

'You say that as if this is over.'

'No… But holidays can't last for ever.'

'That is true. I have to be in London at the end of the week for an industry awards thing.'

'Are you up for something?'

He shook his head. 'Not me this year. I'm presenting an award and I need a date. Are you, by any chance, free on Friday, Miss Forbes Scott?'

'I…' She cleared her throat. 'You're a celebrity, James. There will be cameras there, interest in who you're with.'

'Interest in me is focussed on the hotel at the moment.' His inbox was full of emails from reporters wanting to know how he was feeling about it being back in family hands. 'The lifestyle magazines are full of archive photographs from its glory days. Pictures of film stars, politicians, aristocrats from around the world.'

'I think you'll find that the Forbes Scott name would trump that.'

'You could change it to Chloe Harrington.'

There was one of those moments that sometimes happened in crowded places, when, for a split second, everything fell silent.

Then someone laughed, the clink of crockery being moved, the gentle pop of a cork and Chloe let out a breath that she hadn't been conscious of holding.

'That's a bit extreme, don't you think?' she managed. 'Just to go to a party.'

'I was thinking of something rather more long term.'

'There's no rush,' she said and, because she didn't want this to develop into a conversation that required an answer she wasn't ready to give, 'Why don't you take Hugo as your guest? It would not only show a united family front, but it would be a chance for him to meet industry professionals on this side of the Atlantic.'

'Yes…' James was no longer looking at her, but at the empty glass in his hand. 'I'll ask him,' he said, signalling the waiter, 'but right now I'm going to have a brandy. Would you like something?'

She shook her head. 'Shall we take the bus trip tomorrow?' she asked, changing the subject. 'And perhaps, afterwards, we could check out the *bouquinites*. It's been an age since I've rummaged for a book bargain.'

He thought about it for a moment then nodded and said, 'Why don't we go for it and top it off, literally, with an evening in the champagne bar at the top of the Eiffel Tower?'

'Not a chance.' The joke had been feeble, but they had moved safely on from name-changing talk. It wasn't just that it was too soon… 'That really is a tourist trap too far. And don't tell me that you've never been to the top of the tower, James Harrington, because I won't believe you.'

He held up his hands, found a smile. 'You've got me. Choose whatever you like for tomorrow evening and I'll do my best to deliver.'

'Truly?' She reached across the table and took his hand. 'Then I choose to stay in while you cook for me the way you used to. If that should happen to involve a glass of champagne, I would be extra happy.'

'Your happiness is all I care about,' he said, holding her with a long, steady look until the waitress arrived with the bill for the drinks and the photograph. He paid her, adding a tip, then picked up the photograph and looked at it.

They looked so ordinary as they'd smiled for the camera. Just another happy couple out on a date without a thing in the world to trouble them.

'One for the family album,' he said, sliding it into his pocket as the boat settled back against the pier.

'Let me give you another one, James.'

Chloe had been trying to find the right moment for this, aware that it was an emotional minefield, one she'd shied away from when they were alone. Now he'd given her the perfect opening and she fumbled with the clasp of her bag, finger shaking a little as she took out a small leather folder.

'I found these copies today; they're for you,' she said, offering it to him.

He looked at her for a long moment before he opened it.

On one side was a scan of their daughter at twenty weeks. On the other there was a close-up of their newborn infant, moments after she'd been placed in her arms.

'Eloise…'

He touched the precious images, looking at them for a long moment. Then he looked up and, as she saw the struggle he was having to hold back feelings that he couldn't allow to spill over, she wished she'd been braver.

Wished they were somewhere private so that she could hold him. So that he could let the tears fall.

'I'm sorry. I should have waited.'

He shook his head, stood up.

The cruise was over, the boat was emptying, and he helped her into her coat, hailed a taxi, walked her to the door of the apartment.

It wasn't that he didn't speak, just that the few words he said to thank the staff as they left the boat, to tell the driver where to take them, had nothing to do with her. With them.

He keyed in the door code but when he didn't follow her inside, she said. 'Are you okay?'

'I'm fine, but I need to be on my own for a while.'

His touch to her arm was a gentle reassurance that it wasn't about anything she'd done, but as he walked away she wondered if she should follow him. As if sensing her hesitation, he turned, nodded. 'Go in. I won't be long.'

* * *

Jay walked to the river, bought coffee from a late-night stallholder and sat on a bench. Moments later an old homeless man shuffled along and sat beside him.

He asked him if he could buy him a cup of coffee, maybe a burger.

The stallholder shook his head, said, 'Don't give him any money, or he will drink it.'

Jay nodded, and they sat together for a while in silence until, unbidden, the old guy started to tell him how his wife had got cancer and died. How grief had driven him to drink, his son had been taken in foster care and he'd lost his house. A justification of how he'd ended up sleeping rough.

'What happened to you, son?' he asked, assuming he was on the same downward path.

'Nothing,' he said. Whether the old man was telling the truth scarcely mattered. Compared to him, he was the luckiest man alive. 'I'm absolutely fine.' He got up to leave. The temptation to take out his wallet and hand over some cash was inevitable, but bearing in mind the stallholder's warning he said, 'Is there anything you need?'

'I could use a coat.'

It was true, the one he was wearing was in rags, and Jay took his off, emptied the pockets into his jacket.

'He'll sell it,' the burger guy warned.

He didn't doubt it, but he handed it over anyway and walked back to the flat.

Chloe stirred, felt the cold emptiness in the bed beside her, heard the soft tapping of fingers on a keyboard.

She'd gone to bed but had stayed awake, fretting, until she heard James come in. He'd gone into the kitchen, switched on the kettle and, finally able to relax, she had drifted off.

It had only been a few days and already she missed being able to reach out and touch him, to know that he was beside her, and she eased herself up on the pillow so that she could see him.

He was sitting at the little table beneath the window, the light from the screen lighting up his face as he worked. He was spending all his time with her but there had to be things that he couldn't pass on to someone else. There was a blog with an army of followers, the book he was working on…

'"My candle burns at both ends, it will not last the night…"' she said.

He turned from the keyboard. There were dark hollows beneath his eyes, but he was smiling. 'I'm sorry. I didn't mean to wake you.'

'It wasn't the keyboard,' she said. 'It was your

absence. The bed is cold without you. Where did you go?'

'Down by the river. I just needed a walk to clear my head.'

'Did it work?'

'Yes,' he said. 'It did. I'll take this through to the other room.'

'There's no need,' she said, swinging her legs out of the bed. 'I'm going to make a cup of tea. But just so you know, we don't have to gallivant all over Paris as if all the attractions will be gone in a fortnight. I'm perfectly happy staying in while you work.'

He looked as if he was about to say something about the world and how it had ended for them once before, but he let it go.

'I'm just about done here, but a cup of tea would be very welcome.'

She put the kettle on, cut brioche to make toast while it boiled, and added a pot of marmalade James had bought in the food hall at Galeries Lafayette to the tray.

He smiled appreciatively when she carried it through and joined her when she climbed back into the warmth of the bed.

'Midnight snacks. It's like being back at school.'

'More like four in the morning snacks. And you still have homework, apparently.'

'There's a saying, Chloe, that a man who loves his job never works a day in his life.'

'Confucius.'

'I'm sorry?'

'It was Confucius who said it.' She bit into the toast, relishing the mingled warmth of brioche, butter and the sharp orange tang of the conserve. 'I need to find something that I love that much.'

'Not bedmaking?' he teased. But then he said, 'I didn't realise it at the time, but you never talked about what career you had in mind after school, university. But maybe university wasn't in the plan?'

'I've no idea. It wasn't something I ever discussed with my father. I didn't actually go to school until I was eleven years old, when my mother insisted that I needed a social group.'

'I never knew that. I assumed you'd always been at St Mary's. You were a straight-A student.'

'I had tutors. My mother was brought up to run a country house, be the perfect hostess, but no one had cared much about her education and her ignorance used to irritate my father. He was determined that I would be able to hold my own in every aspect of life.'

'Hence the gallery tours,' he said, lifting the tray to the floor before rolling onto his side so that he was looking at her.

'Among other things. As my father's only heir, it would be my responsibility to keep his legacy intact. I had to account for every penny I spent from the moment I was given an allowance. He fined me if I couldn't balance my books.'

'Unbelievable.'

'It only happened once,' she said. 'I'm a fast learner. And I'm grateful for that lesson every day of my life.'

'You could have done anything, Chloe. You still can. You could take a degree now, as a mature student. I'd support you.'

'There's only one thing I want from you, James, and you don't have to do a thing.' She ostentatiously sucked a smear of marmalade off her thumb.

'A lady would have left that to me.'

'If I'd wanted to be a lady, I would have married the earl-in-waiting,' she said, pushing him onto his back and straddling him. 'Right now, all you have to do is lie back and think of England.'

'Where's your coat?' Chloe asked as they prepared to leave the apartment.

'Last night I gave it to a man who didn't have a home, let alone a coat.'

She raised an eyebrow. 'You gave a homeless man your cashmere coat?'

'It only takes one thing to throw us off balance, a single missed step.'

'And you thought how easily it could have been you?' she asked. Then, 'No. Me. You thought it could be me.'

'We're all one step away from the park bench.'

'That was a seriously head-clearing walk.'

'I take it your father would not approve?'

'He has a charitable foundation, but I imagine he would have thought such a gesture quixotic.'

'Quixotic?'

'Romantic, then.'

'A coat is just a coat, Chloe, and I promise you, my head was never clearer.'

She linked her arm with his. 'I'm fine with romantic. It was a good thing to do but we are going to have to make a stop and replace it or you are going to freeze to death on top of that bus.'

Half an hour later, suitably coated, scarfed and gloved, they were waiting for the hop-on/hop-off bus at the stop near the Sorbonne.

'Are we crazy doing this?' Chloe asked, stamping her feet and looking up at the low clouds. Then, realising that James was engrossed in something on his phone, she made an irritated growling noise. 'I'm sorry. Am I disturbing you?'

'What?' He looked up. 'How do you feel about getting out of Paris for a day or two, Chloe?'

'Somewhere warm?' she asked, hopefully.

'No warmer than here but, since you're getting picky about the more obvious tourist venues, I thought we could hire a car tomorrow and take a trip out to Thoiry to see the light show at the zoo.'

'Oh...' She'd thought he was working, but he'd been looking at places to take her.

'Oh, great? Or, oh, that's the dumbest idea I've heard this week?' he asked.

'Oh, this holiday thing could get addictive.' This James thing could get dangerously addictive...

'So that's a yes?' he prompted, when her head was stuck on that thought...

'Yes, please. I've heard it's absolutely magical.'

'Right answer. I've booked tickets for tomorrow evening and a suite in a nearby château, so we won't have to drive back at night.'

Once again only asking her after he'd gone ahead and booked, but before she could say anything, he showed her the picture of a hotel suite furnished in French provincial style.

'Ohmigod, that's gorgeous.'

'Again, right answer.' He smiled, thoroughly pleased with himself. 'The place even has its own vineyard.'

'Er… You do know it's the wrong time of year to visit a vineyard?'

'But not to talk to the *vigneron* or taste the wine. If it lives up to the notes on their website and you like it, I might buy some for the restaurant.'

'What does my opinion have to do with anything?'

He frowned. 'Your opinion has to do with everything. You are part of my life, Chloe.'

She wanted to be part of his life but a cold spot in the pit of her stomach warned her that this was going way too fast.

She wanted to say hold on, wait, but the bus appeared, and they climbed aboard.

James flashed the ticket on his phone over the scanner while she grabbed a couple of earpieces and by the time he joined her on the top deck she was plugging them in, finding the right language, adjusting the sound.

'Do we need these?' he asked.

She ignored his frown. 'Totally. If I'm doing the tour I want to know who did what and when.'

They toured the Île de la Cité, sighed over the damage to Notre Dame, took selfies of themselves with the Arc de Triomphe in the background, but neither of them mentioned the family album.

There was a brief flurry of snow as they

reached the high spot at the Trocadero. The few people who'd braved the top of the bus with them scrambled off at that point, to go and take photographs of the Eiffel Tower.

Alone, they abandoned the headphones and held out for a few more stops before Chloe said, 'I can't feel my cheeks.'

'I can,' James said, holding his gloved hands, still warm from the cup he'd been holding, against them. Thawing her lips with a lingering kiss that heated her in a way that the brandy-laced coffee had signally failed to do. She clutched at his coat, wanting to hold onto the moment, but then a couple of hardy souls joined them on the top deck and James pulled back a little and she laughed.

'What?'

'Your hair…' It was dusted with snowflakes that, as a shaft of sunlight broke through the clouds, sparkled like diamonds and she took a snap before, self-consciously, he raised a hand and vigorously brushed it over his head. It came away wet.

'You were right, *chérie*. I should have bought a hat.'

'No. It was perfect, but right now I'm done with this. I need soup. Something spicy with beans,' she said. 'Actually, make that anything as long as it's steaming hot.'

'Good call.'

Later, thoroughly defrosted, they wandered along the Seine near Notre Dame, browsing the *bouquinites*. The booksellers had been a feature of the area since the middle of the sixteenth century, but had taken up permanent residence, with their green boxes, in the late nineteenth century and now, as well as vintage books, sold prints and magnets to the tourists.

'What are you looking for?' Chloe asked.

'I collect old cookery books, but I'm also hoping to find something for Sally for Christmas.'

A chat with one of the stallholders produced an early copy of *The Memoirs of Alexis Soyer* that he was excited to find and, while he was haggling over that, Chloe found a beautiful book with colour plates of art deco interiors and handed it to him.

'That's perfect,' he said. 'Sally will love it.'

'What about Hugo?' she asked, putting down a print before he noticed her interest.

'I have no idea. He's my brother but I was just a kid when he disappeared,' he said as they moved on. 'I know he's been a hugely successful hotelier in the States, but I have no idea what interests him.'

'Give it time, James.'

'Time is the one thing we never have. He's been so wrapped up in restoring the hotel, and I have so much on myself. There hasn't been much time to get close.'

'You should organise something that you can do together. Is he into sport?'

'He used to play cricket at school, but they don't play a lot of that in New York.'

'Or in the winter in England. What about football? Can you get tickets to a match?'

'I could, but actually he and Dad were big rugby fans. I remember Dad taking him to watch England play France just before he died. Mum tried to persuade Nick to take him to a match, but it never happened.'

'It sounds as if you've found, not only the perfect gift, but a chance to connect outside work.'

'That is a brilliant idea. I'll get tickets for one of the Six Nations matches at Twickenham.' He checked the fixture list on his phone. 'There is nothing like the sound of fifty thousand voices singing "Swing Low Sweet Chariot" to remind a man that he's English.' He removed his gloves, propped his elbows on the Pont Neuf bridge and clicked away for a minute. 'All done.'

'Wonderful. You'll have a lovely day.'

'It'll be better if England win, but I heard what you said about talking to him, Chloe.' He turned and leaned back against the curve of the ancient stone. 'I called him yesterday and opened up to him about what happened to us.' He glanced at her. 'I hope that's okay?'

'Of course it is. It's your story, too… What did he say?'

'Not much, to be honest. He just listened.'

'I like the sound of Hugo. The world needs more people who know how to listen,' she said, straightening and signalling to a taxi that was dropping people off. 'You'll get there, but right now I think it's time for a little fun.'

He opened the car door. 'Fun?'

'You can wipe that smile off your face, James Harrington,' she said, ducking into the warmth of the cab. 'We're going to be out of Paris for a couple of days and after that you have to go back to London.' The cab driver looked back. 'Rue Coquillière,' she told him. 'DeHillerin.'

'Oh, kitchen fun!' The grin splitting James's face was so wide that he looked exactly like the boy she'd fallen in love with. The boy who'd treated food as if he were an artist, his ingredients the palette he used to create his masterpieces.

Not that they had all been masterpieces. There had been some spectacular disasters, but his passion, his enthusiasm had never been dented by failure. He'd gone for it one hundred per cent.

'Have I said how much I love you?'

'What you're feeling isn't love,' she told him.

'It's anticipation of the culinary equivalent of a trip to Disney.'

'We should do that, too.' The grin, impossibly, widened. 'I'll wake you with a kiss in Sleeping Beauty's castle and we'll live happily ever after.' He reached across the seat to take her hand. 'What do you say, Chloe?'

'I'd say no, thank you, and if you'd read the original story, you might not be so keen on that scenario, either.'

'Is it one of the gruesome ones?'

'They are all pretty gruesome. That one is just plain nasty.' Right down to the stolen babies.

She shivered and James, assuming that she was cold, put an arm around her. Clearly he hadn't heard the clear no, and she felt guilty as she leaned into him, accepting the comfort.

CHAPTER EIGHT

'IT'S NOT GOING to snow,' Jay said.

They were headed out of Paris on the A14, planning to book into the château first, have lunch and then head out to the zoo later for the light show.

'The forecast says snow.'

'The forecast said that any snow is going to fall east of Paris. We're heading west.'

'The sky says different.'

Jay looked across at her, not bothering to hide his amusement. 'Are we having our first argument over the weather forecast?'

'I'm not arguing,' she said. 'I'm merely stating the obvious.'

'I'd forgotten how stubborn you can be,' he said.'

'Only when I'm right.'

'Okay,' he said, 'you may have a point, but this is a major road and we're not in England where half an inch of snow brings the country to a halt and you know what?'

'Never met him.'

He grimaced. 'I can imagine a lot worse things than being snowed in with you, Smarty-Pants, but for now the road is dry and we should soon be at the turning for the château. Forget the weather and look out for that.'

'Yes, sir.' She threw a mock salute and, when he rolled his eyes, she said, 'I haven't forgotten how bossy you can be.'

Before he could object, they reached the turning and, since it was a while since he'd driven on the right-hand side of the road, he had to concentrate on exiting the dual carriageway.

'This is so pretty,' Chloe said as the road narrowed, and they travelled through countryside dotted with small vineyards. Twisting and turning to look at the farmhouses they passed until they reached the outskirts of a large village.

He edged the car through the busy square where a market was in progress.

'Oh, look, it's a *brocante*, James. Can we stop?'

It wasn't what he'd planned, and he had no idea what she thought she'd find in a village flea market, but until now he was the one coming up with all the suggestions. This was the first time she'd asked him for anything.

'Of course we can stop, just promise not to buy anything that won't fit in the car.'

'Spoilsport.'

'Okay, you can buy whatever you like, but you're going to have to figure out how to get it home.'

Home. The word brought a smile to his face. He was living in a one-bedroomed flat on top of the restaurant. It would do as a temporary measure, but he'd find somewhere bigger for them as soon as they were married. Somewhere with a garden.

He found a place to park on the edge of the village and as they walked back, hand in hand, he felt as if they were finally putting the tensions left over from the past behind them. Moving on.

It was a Christmas *brocante*, with a lot of decorations on sale. Willow wreaths, hand-made wooden and felt tree decorations. Boxes of old glass baubles—the kind that smashed if you dropped them.

On one stall he found a snow globe with some age to it.

'My mother had one of these,' he said. 'I wonder if it's still at the house, or if Nick got rid of everything.'

'I'm surprised he didn't sell it. The house.'

'It's in the hotel grounds. It would have been the estate manager's house in the days when the hotel was a private mansion. I assume that Hugo will live there. Or maybe a manager if he decides to put one in. The chances are he'll go back to New York.'

'You, Sally and Hugo should get together and go through everything. There will be photographs, old school reports, birthday cards and maybe even your mother's snow globe.'

'Maybe, but I'll buy this anyway.' He gave it a shake so that the snow swirled around the wintry scene. 'I'll keep it on my desk to remind me of the day it didn't snow.' He held out his hand as if to demonstrate. 'Oh, look, I think that's the sun,' he said, looking up at the sky where there was a glimmer of light behind the clouds.

'Barely,' she said, before turning to examine a huge old mirror in a gilded frame that had seen better days. 'If I had a mantelpiece, I'd buy this.'

'It would have to be a big mantelpiece,' he said, 'and I'd need a bigger hire car.'

'True. This is more my size,' she said, picking up an old art deco cup and saucer and examining the pottery mark stamped on the bottom.

'What use is one cup?' he asked.

'It's pretty and vintage cups and saucers are collectible, James. This is probably the last of a set that has been in someone's family for generations. They would only have been brought out on special occasions.'

She haggled with the man running the stall

and then, when it was safe in bubble wrap, she handed the bag to him.

'Give it to Sally. It will go with the book you bought her.'

About to protest that he should have paid for it, he had a better thought. 'You can give it to her yourself at the Christmas party.'

'I don't want to come to London, James.'

'Because your parents will be there?' He took her arm. 'It'll be all right,' he said. 'Once we're married, they won't be able to touch you.'

Her answer was drowned out by a brass band striking up close by them, playing carols. He put a note in the collecting tin and, as they wandered on, he began to see things through Chloe's eyes.

Not unwanted junk, but family history.

There was an overstuffed leather chair, worn on the arms where it had been rubbed by countless hands. Or one set of hands countless times through a long life.

'That definitely won't fit in the car, James,' Chloe said, when he sat down to check it for comfort.

'I could have it delivered.' He took a photograph with his phone and asked the seller for his card. 'It would look great in the ground-floor club bar at L'Étranger,' he said, when she looked askance at him.

He left Chloe turning over some old linens and

wandered back to the mirror. They didn't have anywhere to put it now, but one day they would. A mantelpiece in a house with a garden…

He called a friend with a van to organise a pickup, sent him pictures of both items and then paid for the mirror and the chair.

He was looking at a small dark blue vase with a gilded panel of white roses when Chloe found him.

'I get it,' he said, showing it to her. 'It's all about the history. Who owned this? Who gave her the *I love you* flowers she put in it? A lover? A man she was married to for fifty years? Her children…?'

'You are such a romantic.'

'Guilty as charged, ma'am.'

The stallholder, sensing her moment, suggested a price that was undoubtedly more than the vase was worth, but he didn't haggle.

'Now our story is part of it, too,' he said, when she'd wrapped it and handed it to him. 'A memory of a day spent together in a French village that I will fill with white roses on the anniversary of this day every year.'

Chloe blinked. 'You'd better put a reminder in your phone.'

'I'm wounded that you have so little faith.'

'Okay,' she said. 'Here's a little test. When is my birthday?'

'Very soon. The twenty-eighth of November,' he said, without hesitation. 'I made you a cake.'

'It was in the shape of a book. And you sent me roses. Yours is in April. The twelfth. I made you a cake, too, but nothing fancy.'

'Lemon drizzle. And you gave me a first edition of Escoffier's *Guide Culinaire*.'

For a moment neither of them moved, then Chloe cleared her throat and said, 'There is so much pretty china here.'

'You see a lot in charity-shop windows. It's sad, but who uses cups and saucers in the age of the mug?'

'Only the Queen and hotels.' She looked at him. 'And tea rooms.'

She picked up a pink, white and gold cake stand and held it up for him to see. 'Is your afternoon-tea service going to be all spare, minimalist white china, or can you imagine using this?' she asked. 'Tables laid with beautiful vintage china, every person drinking their Darjeeling or Earl Grey out of something original. Individual.'

'It's a lovely idea,' he said, 'but is it dishwasher safe?'

'Not a chance,' she said, 'but who cares? You'll employ some very careful person to wash it.'

'And you think I'm a romantic.'

'This is romance with a USP. Imagine this cake stand filled with pretty little cakes, on your website header. Delicate cups and saucers as bullet points…'

'If I admit that it's a great idea and buy this,' he said, 'will you work with Sally on the design?'

'Me?' She frowned. 'No…'

'But it's perfect, Chloe. You're going to be part of my life and you have such a great imagination. I want you to hunt down the china, manage the tea service for me. You have all the skills for this…' He turned to the stallholder to pay for the cake stand, then said, 'This has been an unexpectedly productive morning. You are going to have so much fun with this.'

'I am not going to do anything of the kind,' she said. 'I am going to have lunch and any talk about tea rooms or business of any kind will give me indigestion.'

The entrance to the château was a couple of miles outside the village. Beyond the gate the lane became an unpaved track winding through woodland, but then they were clear of the trees and beyond a pair of majestic wrought-iron gates stood a pink and white château glowing against a slate sky.

Chloe put out a hand and grabbed James's arm. 'Stop!'

He pulled up between the gates and looked at her. 'What's the matter?'

'Absolutely nothing.' She looked at the wide sweep of the house, its pink walls, white stucco trim, the dormer windows in the roof and steps leading up to the front door and couldn't stop a smile spreading from somewhere deep inside until it consumed her entire body. 'This is the dream house I drew as a child.'

'As in a picture stuck to the fridge door with a magnet, drew?'

She nodded. Then pulled a face. 'Obviously not the fridge door, it was pinned to my cork board by my nanny, but yes, I drew it and coloured it in with crayons.'

'You must have seen a picture of it in one of your mother's magazines. They've been hosting weddings and events for years,' he suggested.

'Maybe,' she agreed, although she knew it had to have been in her nanny's copy of *Celebrity*, which featured weddings of even the marginally famous.

'I have to admit that from here it looks even better in real life than in the online photographs, which, in the age of digital enhancement, has to be a first,' James said. 'Can we go now?'

She nodded. 'But slowly.'

He continued along the drive at a snail's pace, giving her time to look around, take in an ancient cedar on the front lawn, catch a glimpse of the orangery and, beyond the trees, a small lake gleaming leaden under the grey sky.

By the time he'd pulled up at the front of the château, one of the double doors had been thrown open and a couple of French bulldogs were followed down the steps by a slightly flustered woman.

'Welcome to Château Bernier St-Fleury, Mr Harrington, Miss Forbes Scott. I'm Marie Bernier. Call me Marie...' She turned to the dogs. 'Beau, Felix—heel! I'm so sorry.'

They scampered around Chloe, sweet but clearly out of control.

'They were my mother-in-law's dogs,' Marie said. 'I'm afraid she spoiled them.'

Chloe bent to rub a silky ear and its owner immediately rolled over and presented her with his tummy. 'I can understand why. They're adorable.'

'They like you, Miss Forbes Scott. Do you have dogs of your own?'

'Chloe, please. I'd love to have a dog, Marie, but I live in a Paris flat and I'm out at work all day. It wouldn't be kind.'

'And you, Mr Harrington?' she asked as one of the dogs abandoned her for James and he offered him a hand to sniff before rubbing an ear.

'Everyone calls me Jay,' he said, 'and like Chloe I'm a city dweller with a job that keeps me busy for long hours. Maybe in the future,' he said. 'When we have a house with a garden.'

Marie smiled, nodded. 'Of course. But, please, come in out of the cold.'

'Your name is Bernier, like the château?' Chloe said, following her inside while James fetched their bags from the car. 'It was built by your family?'

'My husband's family built it as a summer retreat in the nineteenth century. When my father-in-law died, my husband had to take over the business here. That was nearly twenty years ago.'

'It's a magical place.'

Marie Bernier's smile was wry. 'Unfortunately, Chloe, there was no magic wand to repair the roof and there is so much of it...' She raised a hand in a gesture that took in the extent of it. 'The property market was in a shocking state after the bank crash and the family went into the hospitality and weddings business out of necessity. We hit the market just at the right moment and it has been a great success, but now it is just me.'

'I'm so sorry.'

She shrugged. 'We should be planning our retirement now, but Henri had a stroke and then a series of heart attacks. I know things are hard for the young these days, but I always say to my young couples that they should not take life for granted. No one ever died wishing he'd worked harder.'

She indicated the stairs that rose in an elegant curve from the polished wood floor of the hall.

'I'll take you up to your suite so that you can settle in. There's a fire in the morning room and everything you need to make yourself tea and coffee. We have just one other couple staying to-night but they won't be arriving until much later, so you'll have it to yourselves. Dinner will be served at eight. Just ring if you want anything.'

She opened a pair of doors and gave them a quick tour of the suite that James had shown her on his phone. There was the pretty blue and white bedroom furnished in the French style, a little sitting room through a curved archway and a huge claw-footed bath in a wonderfully romantic bathroom.

'Poor woman,' Chloe said, when Marie had left them alone. She was standing at the window looking out over the garden and James came up behind her and put his arms around her. 'I can't imagine how hard it must be to run this place on her own.'

'She's a strong woman,' he said.

'You're thinking about your mother,' she said.

'And my dad. After Mum died, when we found out what Nick was really like, I blamed her for rushing into a second marriage, but she hated the hotel, blamed the stress of running it for Dad's heart attack. Nick must have seemed like a gift.' He noticed her frown and shook his head. 'It's history. Nothing to be done...' Then something caught his eye and he said, 'Look, Chloe! A swan!'

They watched as it came in to land on the lake, skimming across the water before settling with a shimmy of its tail.

'Did you know that they mate for life?' she said.

'So do gibbons. And angelfish...'

She laughed. 'Angelfish?'

'It's true. Check it out.'

'I believe you,' she said, leaning back into him as he pressed a kiss into her neck.

He was so strong, so sure of himself, of his future. She could go back to London with him, sink into his life the way she was sinking into his arms and know that he'd take care of her. That she'd be safe.

'Are you cold?' he asked, when she shivered.

'A bit. Let's go and have some tea.'

'How were the lights?' Marie said, when they returned from Thoiry later that evening.

'Amazing!' Chloe said. 'Noah's Ark, an incredibly beautiful underwater world and an entire Renaissance procession from the court of Henri IV.'

'Ah, yes. He stayed at the Château de Thoiry. It's a lot older than this one,' she said, with wry smile. 'I'm afraid dinner may be a little late. My chef's wife had a fall and he had to take her to the hospital. She is his assistant and serves—'

James paused, one foot on the stairs. 'Can I help?'

'Help?' She shook her head. 'You are a guest,' she objected.

'I'm also a chef. Give me a minute and I'll be with you.' He didn't wait for an answer but bounded up the stairs.

'Really, he does not have to do this,' Marie said, clearly concerned about the reputation of her château.

'You needn't worry. He's really very good. He has a restaurant in London.'

'London...?' She repeated the word as if astonished that anyone in England could cook.

'He trained in Paris.'

'Oh... That is why he speaks such excellent French. As do you, Chloe.'

'Thank you, Marie. I spent a lot of my childhood in France and I've lived here for a long time.'

She smiled, but then remembered their conversation. 'It is kind of him, Chloe, but he'll be in the kitchen working, instead of in the dining room with you. No, I'll manage.'

'Show me,' Chloe said.

The dining room was a large and elegant room with French windows that in the warm weather would open out onto a terrace. A long, dark table with a magnificent silver epergne at its centre had been laid for four with heavy silverware and fine glasses that gleamed in the light from two chandeliers.

Unfortunately, despite the fire that had been lit in the hearth, it wasn't very warm.

'It's lovely in the spring and the summer,' Marie assured her. 'The windows open onto the terrace and the lake. Our other guests are here to look us over as a wedding venue…' The strain was beginning to show and Marie, despite her determination to soldier on, was close to tears. 'The rehearsal dinner in here. The reception in the orangery…'

'It's beautiful,' Chloe said, putting an arm around her. 'I can see how it will be in the spring and so will your other guests when you show them but, since there will only be four of us this evening, perhaps we could find somewhere a little cosier?'

She frowned. 'Cosier?'

'Is there a table in the kitchen?'

She bridled. 'We have a commercial kitchen for guests.'

'But you have a family kitchen?'

'Well, yes, but that isn't, I couldn't possibly...'

'Let me see.'

At her insistence, Marie led her through the hall to an old-fashioned family kitchen. On one wall was a huge dresser loaded with china and copper pans. There were herbs drying on a pot rack hanging from the ceiling and a range oven that was throwing out blissful warmth. And in the centre of the room stood a solid wooden table that looked as if it had been there for a hundred years.

'Marie, this is perfect. I'll just go and wash up and then I'll come and help you set up.'

She met James in the hall.

'I'm sorry. This was supposed to be the perfect romantic evening,' he said, 'but she was clearly about to crack.'

'I love that you stepped up. I love you.' Before he could even think of a response to that, she kissed him. 'The dining room is an ice box. We're cooking and eating in the family kitchen. I'll be down to help as soon as I've washed up.'

Jay, aware that he was grinning like a loon, watched Chloe run up the stairs but then, as headlights swept across the glass panels on either side of the door, Marie appeared, back in control and looking every inch the chatelaine.

'James... I am indebted to you. To you both.'

'On the contrary, Marie, believe me when I say I have every reason to be grateful to you. The kitchen is through here?'

'It is. The menu is on the blackboard. There are no special dietary requirements.'

'Then look after your guests and leave the food to me.'

He was checking the menu against the ingredients when Chloe joined him. 'What have we got?' she asked, reaching for an apron and tying it around her waist.

'A soufflé *Suissesse*, smoked salmon pâté, duck with glazed parsnips, cheese, and then a tarte Tatin with quenelles of home-made vanilla ice cream. The pâté and the ice cream have been prepared.'

'That helps, but you don't have time to make a tarte Tatin from scratch. The pastry needs to rest for an hour.'

He smiled. 'Since when were you the expert?'

'I don't just wait tables in the bistro. I help out in the kitchen when I'm needed and tarte Tatin is a staple.'

He held her gaze for a moment, then said, 'Marie has already made the pastry, or we'd have had to improvise. Since you're such an expert I'll leave you to peel the apples and line the dish with the pastry while I make the caramel so that we can get it in the oven.'

'Yes, chef.'

Ten minutes later, the tarte was ready and, once it was in the oven, Chloe peeled parsnips while James made a start on the bechamel sauce for the soufflé.

Marie joined them and began setting up the table for four.

'You should eat with us, Marie,' James said.

'Impossible. You will need someone to serve.'

'You're on your own here?' Chloe asked, concerned.

'The bookings came in late and the girl who usually helps is away. I could have called someone else, but I thought with Claud and his wife here I could manage.'

'It's the butter-side-down law.'

Marie laughed. 'Always. I should have known that once the first thing went wrong today the rest would collapse like a house of cards. It is always the way.'

'Something else has gone wrong?' Chloe asked. It wasn't just the missing chef and his wife?

'A wedding cancellation. A bride with cold feet. Or maybe it was the groom.'

'I imagine you had already put a lot of work into the planning.'

'It's not about the work, and I keep the deposit in the event of a late cancellation,' she said, 'but it always makes me a little sad. All those hopes and dreams for a future that will never happen.'

'They might get back together,' James said, looking at her. 'People do.'

'Yes, they do…' She desperately wanted this to work, but he suffered from selective hearing… 'Lay another place, Marie. We'll eat like family. You can relax and talk to your guests about their wedding plans and we'll take our time between courses so that we can all eat together.'

'Is there anything I can do to help?' she asked.

'Open a bottle of your finest white wine?' James suggested.

She went through to the cold room and returned with a bottle that immediately dewed in the warmth of the kitchen, opened it and poured them each a glass.

'To rare and special guests.' She raised her own glass to them. 'Always welcome. *A vôtre santé!*'

CHAPTER NINE

Chloe was aware that Fiona, the Scottish bride-to-be, had been looking at James all evening. She'd done her best to distract her but, finally, she said, 'Your face is so familiar, Jay. Have you ever been to Edinburgh?'

'Sadly, no,' he said. 'I just seem to have one of those faces. Can I tempt you to another slice of tarte Tatin?'

She held up a hand. 'Don't! I have a wedding dress to shrink into, but I have to say, Marie, that if Jay is your stand-in chef, I cannot imagine what the first division is like. That tarte has to be on our wedding menu.'

Marie looked at James, clearly embarrassed, and he said, 'I can take no credit for the wonderful pastry. The addition of the almonds was a lovely touch, Marie, and one I will borrow if I may?'

Marie blushed. 'It was my mother's recipe. I would be delighted to share it with you.'

'You are definitely having your wedding here, then?' Chloe asked, heading Fiona off before she could return to thoughts of where she might have seen James.

She looked questioningly at Sean. He shook his head, but his indulgent smile said yes. She threw her arms around him. 'You are my angel!'

Embarrassed, he disentangled himself. 'We came to an event in the grounds here last spring and Fiona hasn't stopped talking about it since.'

'I know how she feels,' Chloe said. 'The château took my breath away when I saw it.'

'Is that why you're here?' Fiona asked, looking from her to James. 'To arrange your own wedding?'

'We haven't got around to a date yet,' James said, reaching out, taking her hand when the silence went on a moment too long, looking at her, holding her with the intensity of his gaze. 'And Chloe can choose whatever location she likes as long as it's soon.'

Fiona gave a happy little sigh. 'Wait until the spring,' she urged. 'You can't imagine how pretty it is here when the blossom is out. I just about died when I saw the wedding pictures on the website.'

'If you'd already seen the château, why have you come now?' Chloe asked, desperate to change the subject. 'It was dark when you arrived and you're leaving so early that you won't see it in daylight.'

'Sean was coming to Paris for a meeting and I begged for a night here so that I could see the inside of the château and take a look at the bridal suite. I wish we could stay longer, but we have to leave at a ridiculously early hour so that he can catch a flight to Frankfurt.' She rolled her eyes, whispered, 'He's a banker.'

'Which is why we must reluctantly leave such great company,' Sean said, getting to his feet. 'Thank you for a wonderful evening, Marie. If I had my way, we'd have our wedding breakfast in here.'

Fiona laughed. 'There's not enough room for eighty guests in here, darling.'

Clearly that was Sean's point, but he smiled. 'Only eighty?'

She gave a little shrug. 'That's the maximum number Marie can seat in the orangery, but we'll have a bigger party in the evening.'

'Of course we will. I won't see you in the morning, Jay, Chloe.' He shook Jay's hand, kissed Chloe's cheek. 'Thank you both for an unforgettable meal.'

When they were gone, Chloe ignored Marie's objections and began to clear the table. James, the consummate professional, had cleaned down as he'd cooked, and the kitchen area only needed a final wipe.

'What time is breakfast?' Chloe asked.

'Whenever you want it,' Marie said. 'There is no one else booked into your room so you can stay as late as you like. And I will refund the cost of your stay.'

'Marie…'

'I mean it. Without you I would have lost that wedding booking.'

'She's right, Chloe. You were born to run a big house,' James said as they made their way upstairs. 'Marie was floundering, not just earlier, but several times during the evening. You kept her going.'

'Only after you had stepped in to save the day.'

'I imagine I volunteered about half a second before you did it for me.'

'Maybe.' Her smile faded. 'She's not managing, is she?'

'Honestly? If I were Sean, I'd be encouraging Fiona to look for somewhere else to hold my wedding but thanks to you they didn't notice that anything was wrong.'

Chloe glanced at him as they reached their room. 'Fiona certainly noticed you, though.'

'Yes. Thanks for the deflection,' he said, sliding his arms around her. 'We make a great team.'

'I can peel a great vegetable,' she agreed.

'It wasn't just the cooking,' he said, 'although that was so like the way it used to be with us.'

'Out of hours in the school kitchen with you

putting out a hand and barking "spatula", or "ginger", and me following orders like a theatre nurse?'

'Like a *sous chef*,' he corrected, then frowned, belatedly catching something in her voice. 'It was good, wasn't it?'

'Yes,' she said, melting a little. 'It was good. And I really enjoyed this evening. It felt real.'

'Real?'

'Yes. Sightseeing, eating out...' She raised a hand in an effort to convey what was missing. 'They're great, but they aren't real life.'

He put his hands on her shoulders and looked down into her face. 'Holidays are part of life, Chloe, and I realised that you needed time to adjust. For us to get to know one another again.' She felt suddenly trapped, but as she pulled away James turned and headed for the bathroom. 'It's going to be perfect,' he called back. 'Just how it used to be.'

'We were children, James. And it wasn't perfect.'

He didn't answer and she followed him.

His hair was standing up in an untidy ruff where he'd pulled his tee shirt over his head and he had his toothbrush in his hand.

He looked at her through the mirror and it was obvious that he hadn't heard her. 'I've been thinking.'

'Steady,' she said, unnerved by his sudden gravity.

He didn't laugh.

'This is important, Chloe. I meant what I said earlier about getting married as quickly as possible. I checked with my lawyer. Once you're my wife, legally your father will have no power over you.' He turned to face her. 'He would never again be able to control you by shutting you away in some discreet private clinic...'

For a moment she couldn't breathe as he touched her deepest fear, but as he reached for her she turned away, bending over the bathtub to fix the plug in place, turning on the water until the gush of it drowned out the sound of a girl begging...

'Can we talk about this tomorrow? The only thing that I want right now is to wallow in this vast bath and wash away the smell of cooking.'

Steam was beginning to rise from the huge claw-footed bath, and she sprinkled in something that filled the room with the scent of a summer meadow—flowers, crushed herbs, new-mown grass—as it bubbled up.

'Will you wash my back?' she asked, turning to face him. 'Or are you too tired?'

He reached behind her and turned off the taps and for a moment she thought that he was going to insist on talking about marriage, London...

'It's not full,' she protested.

'We can top it up when we're ready.' He made a circular motion with his hand, indicating that she should turn around.

'We?'

He raised an eyebrow. 'If I'm going to wash your back thoroughly, I'm going to have to get in with you.'

Relief flooded through her. 'I was hoping you'd say that.'

'I know,' he said, 'and I'm happy to help, but first I'm going to have to undress you, so turn around.'

The absence of the lazy smile he wore when anticipating great sex was oddly disturbing and, as she obeyed him, she felt a flutter of panic beneath her breastbone. But then his breath whispered across the nape of her neck. His lips followed, planting soft, seductive kisses that brought something less than a moan, more than a sigh to her throat as he pulled loose the pin holding her hair so that it fell about her shoulders.

She had been leading this dance.

Since that first crazy time he had always been so careful to let her take the lead in their lovemaking. To show her that whatever they did together was her choice. But the restraint had slipped and the shiver rippling through her was more than desire, heat, lust as he followed the slow journey of her zip down her spine with his lips, pausing only to unclip the roadblock of her bra.

This was deeper, darker, and as her dress, bra, slipped to the floor she tried to turn to him.

'Be still,' he murmured against her ear, cupping her breasts in his hands, teasing her nipples with the tips of his thumbs as he held her against his chest, his arousal nudging her. Then, as she moaned, 'Are you still in a hurry, my love?'

'You can take all the time in the world,' she gasped, 'as long as you keep doing that.'

Because the physical connection between them was as real, as powerful as it had been when they were teens exploring this exciting new world and each touch had been a discovery.

It still was.

What had happened in those first explosive moments after he'd found her was the release of the need, hunger, a sexual energy that had been suppressed through all those missing years. When they were close like this nothing else mattered. It never had...

He didn't have to hold her, she was leaning back into him, rubbing against him, whimpering, begging, building up to a frustrated scream...

'Shh...' he whispered in her ear, one hand low against her belly but tormentingly not low enough. 'You'll make Fiona jealous.'

She swore then and he laughed, still tweaking one rock-hard nipple while sliding his other hand lower, into her tights, her underwear.

Her core was liquid, her legs barely able to hold her, but instead of the release she was begging for, bucking her hips to find his fingertips and achieve with or without him, he moved his hand away, abandoned her breast and began to slowly peel the clinging tights and pants over her hips.

He took his time, his hands spread over her buttocks, fingers, mouth finding every tender spot as he carried them down to her feet until he was on his knees and, at his bidding, she lifted each foot until she was naked.

'You can turn around now, Chloe.'

She turned to face him, quivering with the intensity of her need, her nails digging into his naked shoulders as she clung to him for support, feeling exposed as she never had before.

He leaned forward, placed a row of kisses along the base of her belly. Scarcely breathing, she waited for the touch of his tongue. It didn't come. Instead he looked up at her and said, 'Your turn.'

The bath grew cold as she subjected him to the same slow, agonisingly sweet torture. Arousing him with her fingers, her breasts, her tongue, as he had aroused her. Fighting to curb her own need, drawing out every second to give him the same intensity of sweet agony that he had given her.

His control was awesome, but there came a moment when, with a yell that, if the walls hadn't been a foot thick, would have woken the dead in the nearby churchyard, he picked her up and carried her to bed and, much later, every need satisfied, blissful oblivion.

Jay lay in the darkness and listened to Chloe breathe. He'd felt the exact moment when she'd slipped away into sleep, limbs heavy, utterly sated, wearing the same little smile he'd seen after the first time they'd made fumbling, first-time love. Admitting to feeling a little sore but delighted with herself.

It had been a long day and he should be exhausted but sex left him stimulated, his brain racing. If he'd been at home, charged up like this, he would have gone into the kitchen and started to play with ideas.

He could get on with the book, but the light, the sound of the keyboard, would disturb Chloe.

All he could do was lie in the dark, unable to shut down his mind as it replayed everything that Chloe had said. The things she hadn't said. The missed moments when an answer would

have been life changing but she had changed the subject or diverted him as she had done tonight.

Had she always done that?

Even when they were young, and he was running on about the future? Their life together? She would smile and kiss him, and they would make love, and he'd thought that was her answer. But she had known all along that it was never going to happen.

He hadn't noticed until tonight. But tonight, he'd used the marriage word and in her panic she'd been less than subtle in her attempt to avoid it.

He'd thought to punish her a little for that, keep her on the edge until she was begging him to release her. Take her to that place where she wouldn't have to think about a future that scared her. Give her *la petit mort*…the little death that followed orgasm.

She had begged but he was the one who'd lost, because she had given and given, and he was the one who had died a little.

'Feel free to tell me I told you so.'

Chloe stirred, rolled over. It was late, the room was flooded with light, but not the light you got on a sunny morning, not even a sunny winter morning. It was the kind of light you only got in winter when…

'It's snowed!'

James, hair damp from the shower and already dressed, turned away from the window. 'According to Météo-France,' he said, 'the storm took an unexpected swerve to the west in the early hours.'

'Oh, my . . .'

Grabbing the comforter from the bed, she wrapped it around her and went to join him.

From their window, too far away to see the marks left by animals and birds, the scene stretched away in a sheet of unblemished glittering white across the lawn to the lake.

Every branch of every tree was a tracery of white against a blue sky. The silence was absolute, everything completely still until a wood pigeon took off from a branch in a flurry of snow, startling a whole load of other birds into flight.

'It's so beautiful,' she said, leaning against his shoulder. 'Thank you so much for bringing me here, James. I'll never forget it.'

'I'm not sure it was such a good idea.'

'Well, I did warn you that it was going to snow,' she said. 'I wonder if Fiona and Sean got away safely.'

'I heard them leave just after five this morning.'

'They woke you?'

'No. I heard their car. I'm not used to being

idle,' he said, dismissing the sleepless night as if it were nothing. 'I had a million things going around in my head. Plans for us.'

He turned to look at her and in the brilliant light she could see the faint smudges beneath his eyes. 'Plans?'

'You're right, Chloe. These few days have given us a chance to reconnect, rediscover each other, but it's time to get real.'

She had known this was coming, but she wasn't ready…

'I may have been a little hasty,' she said. 'We should take a snow day.'

'The snow is pretty, but not very deep. Nothing short of a fallen tree across the lane is going to stop us from leaving today.'

She laughed. 'Am I that obvious?'

'You know that I'd happily stay another night if it would make you happy, Chloe, but I have to be in London tomorrow evening. I just hope the weather hasn't affected the trains.'

'Yes, I'm sorry. I'm being selfish…'

She rose on her toes, but her brief kiss became deeper, more intense, and for a moment, as he held her, London, the future, was forgotten. Being with him was all that mattered.

James was the one who pulled away, resting his forehead against the top of her head for a moment. 'It's not too late to change your mind and come with me, Chloe.'

'I thought we'd agreed that I'd just be a distraction,' she said. 'You'll have a much better time with Hugo.'

'I doubt that, but you don't have to come to the awards ceremony.' He lifted his head to look into her eyes, laid his hand against her cheek. 'There's just time for us to be married before Christmas but I need you with me so that we can sort out a civil ceremony. We can do the whole white dress, big party later. Here, in the spring, if you like.'

'If Marie is still in business. I'm not sure she's coping very well.'

'The château will still be here. I'll shut the restaurant and bring my own staff if necessary.' He wasn't smiling; he meant it. Wanted an answer. 'I bought a decoration for you to hang on the family tree, Chloe.'

'Did you? When?' she asked, grabbing any chance to delay this moment.

'At the Christmas fair. You chose the flamingo.'

'I thought you just wanted my opinion.' She was struggling to breathe; the walls were closing in… 'I hadn't realised you'd bought it for me to hang on your tree.'

'It's not my tree, Chloe. It's a family tradition

and I want you to be part of my family. I thought, hoped, that it was what you wanted, too.'

Trapped, cornered into a conversation that she had been avoiding, she clutched at the comforter, holding it like a shield.

'I don't feel adequately dressed for this conversation.'

His thumb caressed her cheek. 'You don't need to be dressed if the answer is yes, Chloe.'

'It's complicated,' she said, through a throat that was suddenly stuffed with cobwebs. 'I'm complicated.'

'We can work through it. Just tell me what is bothering you.'

'You know I love you, James. Finding you, being with you, has been a joy. But moving to London, giving up my life here—'

'You have no life here.'

'Please, James, try to understand…' She took a step towards him, but he was already moving away, and she didn't know how to stop him. How to explain something she didn't understand herself. 'Can we talk about this later?' she pleaded.

'Of course. I'll leave you to get dressed. I have to make a few calls and the messages are piling up and it will be easier working at the table in the morning room.' He picked up his phone, slung his laptop bag over his shoulder but paused in the doorway and looked back. 'I'll have Marie send up a tray for you.'

Her mouth was open to say something, anything to stop him leaving, but all that emerged was a whispered, 'No. Thank you. I'll come down. I need some air.'

And then she was looking at a door that had been closed very quietly.

Jay leaned back against the door he had just closed with such excessive care. Slamming it would serve no purpose, no matter how much he felt like it.

He didn't understand.

He'd been upfront, clear from the start about how he saw their future, and Chloe had seemed happy to go along with his plans. Okay, she hadn't shown any great enthusiasm about joining him in London, but his life was there.

She was fully engaged in their physical relationship. More than engaged. She'd taken the lead when he would have willingly waited, understanding that she might need time.

Maybe he should have waited, because she had shied like a spooked foal at the mention of marriage and if it wasn't to be that, what was it?

'Good morning, Jay.' Marie was regarding him intently. 'You slept well, I hope?'

He straightened. 'Yes, thank you, Marie. We were very comfortable.'

'Chloe is still sleeping?'

'I've left her taking a shower while I get a little work done.'

She lifted a despairing hand. 'Men. They are all the same.' She shook her head, sighed. 'You'll find breakfast laid out in the morning room,' she said, 'but find time to take a walk before you go. Fling a few snowballs. Be young.'

'I'll do my best,' he said, but then as she began to move away, 'Marie...' She waited. 'I have to go to London tomorrow, but I think Chloe might like to stay on here for a day or two. Would that be possible? You mentioned more problems yesterday? There was more than the chef and the cancelled wedding, I think.'

'You're right, but it's nothing that need concern you, Jay. I have no guests booked in until next weekend and I would welcome Chloe's company. She is welcome to stay.'

'You are alone here?'

'The cleaning staff come in every morning when we have guests. Less often between bookings, although it's vital to keep on top of the dust. My sons visit from Paris when they can, but they have important careers, children at school.'

'They must worry about you here on your own.'

'They have been urging me to sell the château and move near them.'

'And you?'

'It's not that easy when it has been your life, but my husband was the *vigneron*. It became his passion.' She smiled fondly at the thought of him, before bringing herself back to the moment. 'I have someone who has taken on the job, but a good vintage requires passion.'

'I understand. Perhaps I can talk to you about your wine before I leave? I was impressed with those you served last night, and I'd like to take some samples back for my sommelier to try.'

'Of course. Tell me when you're ready and I'll take you through to the cave, for a tasting.' She took a step, then paused again. 'I looked you up on the Internet this morning, Jay. Chloe told me that you had a restaurant in London—' she gave a little shrug '—to reassure me, you understand. I am honoured to have had you cook in my kitchen.'

'It was my pleasure, Marie. Cooking and eating in good company is always a pleasure. It was a most enjoyable evening.'

The morning after was anyone's guess.

CHAPTER TEN

CHLOE CLUTCHED THE comforter around her, staring out at the pristine landscape, aware that she'd hurt James, that she was behaving irrationally.

This had been her dream, so what was stopping her from jumping on the train to London? Grabbing the first available date at the register office? Hanging that damn flamingo on the Harrington Christmas tree?

She had to get outside and take a head-clearing walk. Work out what was wrong with her. Why, when her heart was so certain, was her head fighting commitment to the boy she'd never stop loving, to the man he'd become?

She blasted herself awake under the shower, dried her hair and wrapped herself up in her warmest clothes.

A cleaner, polishing the curved wooden handrail of the stairs, excused herself and moved to one side, but Chloe smiled to reassure her. She'd been there when she was meant to be invisible.

'Is Madame Bernier in the kitchen?' she asked.

'No, *madame*, she is giving a wine tasting to one of the guests in the cave.'

'Of course. Thank you.'

She didn't want to wait while coffee cooled, just drank some orange juice, grabbed a croissant and, followed by the dogs, walked across the lawn to the lake. They chased ahead of her, nosed under the snow, begged for her croissant, which she surrendered without a fight. Once under the trees where the snow was thinner, she found sticks that she threw for them to chase.

Letting her head clear, letting go of everything as she laughed at their antics.

A low sun was slanting through the clouds, gleaming pale yellow on the glass front of the orangery, the lake was still, disturbed only by ducks and dab chicks who took to the water in a flurry of indignation when the dogs bounded up, wanting to play.

A single majestic swan.

She brushed snow from a bench and sat down, with the dogs panting from their exertions at her feet, and soaked up the perfect peace.

Jay spent some time in the wine cave with Marie, tasting wines, asking her about the grape variety, the number of bottles produced, all the information his sommelier would need. Marie was very knowledgeable, giving him a tour of the cave.

It began as a distraction from his concern about Chloe and where their relationship was going, but he found himself drawn in by the history of the vineyard, which predated the château. By the process.

He chose half a dozen vintages to take back to London with him but as they emerged he saw the tracks in the snow.

'Chloe has not waited for you, Jay.'

'No…' He took a breath, aware that the next hour would change his life. 'I'll put these in the car and then I'll go and find her.'

'I'll bring you some hot chocolate to warm her while you talk. I suspect you could do with something more bracing,' she said, 'but you will be driving.'

'Coffee will be fine. Thank you.'

She patted his arm and went inside while he put the wine in the car and let the silence settle around him, the peace calm him.

Chloe heard the crunch of snow long before James appeared, offering her a lidded carry-out mug.

'Marie thought you might be cold and sent you hot chocolate.'

'That was kind of her. Thank you.'

He swept the snow from the bench and sat beside her, looking out across the water.

'When do you want to leave?' she asked when he didn't speak.

'I'm ready to go, but you're not coming with me. I've arranged with Marie for you to stay on for a few days.'

Chloe fought down the giddy pleasure that thought gave her and turned to look at him. All she got was his unsmiling profile, the sun gilding the tips of his hair and the outline of his close-cropped beard.

'Why would you do that?' she asked, keeping very still.

'It makes sense,' he said. 'You love it here and I'll be in London.'

'I'll rephrase that,' she said, unable to keep the barest tremor from her voice. 'Why would you do that without talking to me first?'

Clearly taken aback by her tone, he said, 'I thought you'd be pleased.'

'That is beside the point.'

'Is it?' He turned to her. 'What is the point, Chloe? Tell me, because I really don't understand what's going on in your mind.'

But she did.

She finally understood.

'I love you, James, but I can't live with a man who wants to control me. Put me in a box. Make me into some version of me that fits in with his life.'

'What on earth are you talking about?'

His astonishment was real. He had no idea what he'd been doing, she realised, but then it had taken her a while to work out what was bothering her.

It seemed that he needed a demonstration, so she put her hand on his shoulder and in a slightly patronising tone, said, 'You don't have to worry about a thing, Chloe. I'm going to set up a tea room. It'll be the perfect little job to keep you busy while I concentrate on building my empire.'

She opened her hands, palms up in a gesture that invited him to contradict her.

He shook his head, clearly bewildered. 'I can't believe you're thinking like this. I love you, I only want what's best for you, Chloe, to take care of you, protect...'

His voice faltered as she rose to her feet and took a step away from the bench, distancing herself from him because this was hard. Really hard...

'They are the exact same words my father used,' she said, oddly calm as she shattered the dream she'd been cherishing for years. 'Over and over. When he took me out of school he said he was rescuing me...' She swallowed down the memory. 'Isn't that what you thought you were doing when you rushed me out of my apartment?'

'No,' he protested as he came to his feet, but

something had clearly hit home. 'Maybe, but it's not the same.'

'He said them when he forced me to sign the adoption papers. When he'd taken our baby. When he took me to the clinic and left me there for months and months…'

'Chloe, please,' he said, reaching for her, 'this is nonsense…'

'You rushed me out of my flat, James,' she said, backing away, because to touch him, to let him touch her, would make it impossible for her to say the words. And she had to say them before this went any further… 'You rushed me out of my life. It wasn't a great life and I know you were doing what you thought was right. But so, in his twisted way, did he. I escaped that cage, James, and I will not step into another one, no matter how comfortable.'

He recoiled as if she'd hit him and she had to dig her nails into her palms to stop herself from reaching out to grab him, hold him…

'You didn't have to come with me,' he said, fighting to hold back his anger, because she had hurt him. Because he still wasn't hearing what she was saying. 'I didn't drag you kicking and screaming down the stairs. The only screaming I heard was you begging for more.'

'I asked you to leave,' she reminded him, 'but you stayed.'

'I couldn't leave you in that place!'

'It wasn't your choice.' Was that her speaking in that calm voice? She felt like an onlooker, someone listening to a woman she didn't know… 'I went with you, James, because I never stopped loving you. It was never a fun fling. It was real, to-the-ends-of-the-earth love. It always will be—'

'Then whatever I've done, or you think I've done, we can fix this!'

'But last night,' she continued, as if he hadn't spoken, 'when I tried to explain, you held my shoulders and spoke to me as if I were a wilful child.' She looked him in the eyes, her heart breaking at his bewilderment. 'He did that.'

'No! I am nothing like your father.' He dragged his hands through his hair, searching for the words to convince her. 'I held you because while you were pulling me so close physically, I could feel you slipping away from me and I was so scared of losing you again.'

'You never lost me. I was always yours.'

'So why was it that any time I mentioned London, or marriage, you changed the subject, or distracted me? You do a very good distraction, Chloe…'

'It was real, James. Every touch, every kiss…'

'Was it?' He shook his head. 'I finally realised what you were doing last night. I'd thought that here, away from Paris, you might begin to see our future...'

'Thinking for me,' she said.

'Thinking of you,' he said, 'but clearly you can't see that.' And this time it was James stepping back, his face the colour of stone. 'Your father is still controlling your life, Chloe. Until you confront that, deal with that, you will never have a future. With me. With anyone. You will always be alone, hiding in a damp, cold room, working as a maid.'

It was a cruel thing to say, meant to inflict pain and it did, but she understood his need to retaliate.

And he was right.

He'd appeared out of the blue like a knight in shining armour, lifting her clear of the rut she'd worn so deep that she'd lost sight of the horizon, of a future. Now it was there, shining before her...

'I won't go back to that,' she promised him. Promised herself. 'Thank you for finding me. For a wonderful week. I will never forget it, or you. But whatever happens next has to be my choice.'

She felt she should offer him her hand. A final gesture, but if he took it, she knew how hard it would be to let go. And if he rejected it...

'Drive carefully, James.'

He frowned. 'You are staying?'

'No, but I'll make my own way back to Paris.'

'That's stu—'

He caught himself, maybe imagining for himself how it would be with the two of them sitting in silence on the drive back. So different from the teasing journey the day before. Exploring the *brocante*, sparking ideas off each other. Then there would be the awkwardness of another night in the same small apartment. Or of James insisting he move into a hotel.

'I'll arrange a car for you.'

'No, James. Thank you, but I can get back to Paris by myself.'

His mouth tightened at this further rejection, but he said, 'I am aware of that. You clearly weren't listening when I said that you could do anything. Be anything.' He took a breath. 'It's nothing to do with control. I brought you here and it's my responsibility to see you safely home.'

'You are the one not listening, James. If this was sex and I said no—'

'Stop!' He was white with anger. 'It is not the same.'

'I was making a point.'

'It's made,' he said. 'You want to make your own way back to Paris. Am I allowed to ask if you have money?'

'Yes, all I need,' she assured him. 'And I will contact Julianne at the hotel, thank her for giving you my address and tell her that I've been to London to talk to an old school friend about a job, but that I have decided to stay in Paris.'

Something that, if she'd been thinking more clearly, she could have done at the time, but maybe she'd wanted to believe James's concern about scandal. Wanted to be carried away. But life was not a prettied-up fairy tale.

'That's it, then,' James said and this time there was no lift on the last syllable, no suggestion of a question. 'Nothing more to be said. I'll go straight to the Gard du Nord and take the first available seat on the Eurostar this afternoon.'

'I'll text you when I've moved my things from Louis's apartment.'

She could see him fighting the need to tell her to stay for as long as she liked, and she died a little inside. She had never meant to hurt him like this…

'If you need anything, any time, you know where I am. But then you always did.' He raised a hand in a heartbreakingly helpless gesture and, his voice cracking, he said, 'I love you, Chloe.'

He didn't wait for her to respond, but as he walked quickly back across the snow she whispered, 'I love you, James Harrington. Always have. Always will.'

A few minutes later, Chloe heard the car driving away and, unwilling to return to the château, she began to walk around the lake. She had reached the orangery when Marie found her.

'You've been out here too long, *chérie*. You'll catch your death.'

'Unlikely in this clean fresh air,' she said, although the dogs had long ago deserted her for the warmth of the kitchen. 'Did James ask you to come and check on me?'

'He was very unhappy to leave you here, I think?'

'I'll take that as a yes.' She sighed, stopped walking. 'He's unhappy because I won't go to London with him, Marie.'

'Is there a reason for that?'

'Not one that he understands.'

She gave a little shrug. 'It is just a few days, yes? He has arranged for you to stay here until he returns.'

'He told me,' she said, 'but it's not possible. We've split up.' Saying the words out loud hit her with the reality of what she'd done, and hot tears began to run unchecked down her frozen cheeks. 'Sorry. So stupid…'

She scrambled in her pocket for a tissue and Marie put her arms around her, held her close, murmuring soft comforting words in French, until she pulled away, drew in a long shuddering breath and blew her nose.

'It was my decision,' she said. 'James is not to blame for what happened. He would have taken me back to Paris but…'

'It would have been an uncomfortable journey. But it's very sad. You seemed to be so close. When I saw you working together it was as if you were two parts that had found one another and together make a whole. And when he looked at you…' She sighed. 'You have been together long?'

'We met when we were very young. My parents did not approve and split us up.'

'But you found each other again.'

'By chance. I was working in a hotel. He was staying there…'

'That is so romantic!'

'Honestly? I took to my heels and ran away, but he found me.'

'Like a movie!'

Despite everything, Chloe laughed. 'Maybe. A bit. The love is still there, the passion is as strong as when we were teenagers. James wanted to whisk me off to London, to marry me before Christmas, but it seems that I have unresolved issues. Maybe we both do.'

'Can you resolve them?' Marie asked hopefully.

'This isn't a movie, Marie. Some things are

not meant to be. Sadly, I will be leaving as soon as I can organise a taxi to the nearest railway station. Or maybe there's a bus?'

'You will go nowhere today, *chérie*,' she said firmly. 'I will make us something comforting for lunch and then you can put your feet up in front of the fire. You can weep, or sleep, or talk if you feel like it. Give your heart a little time to catch its beat. Tomorrow will be soon enough to pick yourself up and start again.'

'I can't afford—'

'As my guest,' Marie said, dismissing the notion that she should pay. 'I tried to refund Jay for last night after he stepped in so gallantly to help us, but he wouldn't hear of it. We spent such a good hour in the cave, where he tasted our best vintages, asked so many questions about the vineyard…' There was a wistfulness in her voice, then a wry smile as she said, 'He won't want to serve it in his restaurant and be reminded of this morning…'

'I doubt he'll let that cloud his judgement. He's always been driven. I don't think, until now, I realised how much.'

'His issues? It was clear that Fiona had recognised him from somewhere and a quick search on the Internet revealed him to be the youngest chef ever to be awarded a star…' She waved a hand, fanning her face. 'The embarrassment!'

'There's no need to be embarrassed. He could have been a short-order cook in a pub for all you knew.'

'You are both so kind… Please stay, Chloe. At least for tonight. A small enough thank you.'

The thought of travelling back to Paris, to the empty apartment, was not appealing and she surrendered to the temptation. 'Thank you, Marie, but can I take a rain check on the pity party? There has been too much weeping in my life. What I'd really like is to see the château. From cellar to attic.'

Marie gave her a long look, as if uncertain whether she would break down somewhere awkward, and Chloe turned to the orangery.

'Shall we start here? Tell me all about the weddings that have taken place here, the events…' Marie shrugged, produced a bunch of keys and opened the door. Explained how the room was set up for weddings, how each one was individually tailored to the couple's wishes.

'How much help do you have?' Chloe asked as they walked back to the château. 'The detail you put into each wedding, each event, must involve a huge amount of work.'

'There is an army of young people who come in on the day, but I have to admit that the joints are stiffer these days. The recovery time from the pressure of weddings and events gets a little longer each time. And as I was telling James, my sons are eager for me to move to Paris to be nearer to them.'

'I can understand that. With this beautiful château and a solid business, you'll be inundated with offers.'

'Maybe. But my husband and I put our hearts and soul into making the château viable.' Marie paused to look up at the pretty pink and white facade, love for the place shining from every line in her face. 'I can only let it go when I'm sure I've found someone who will love it as I do. Someone who can see beyond the fantasy to the hard work it takes to maintain it. I thought I had, but they changed their mind.'

'You heard yesterday?'

Marie nodded as they reached the door to the mud room and kicked off their boots, hung up their coats.

'You said you worked in a hotel, Chloe. What do you do there?'

'Housekeeping. I wait tables and help out in the kitchen at a bistro. Cleaning work.'

'Odd jobs for one as expensively educated as you.'

'Expensively?'

'You have the poise, the accent and it was clear at dinner last night that you have a wide knowledge of the arts, Chloe.'

'Expensive but disjointed. Like my life. I have to go back to Paris, Marie, but when I've sorted things out there would you consider giving me a job? A sort of internship? You don't have to pay me. I'm not afraid of hard work and I'll do anything for my bed and board and the chance to learn everything about how this works.'

'You would like to buy the château?' she asked hopefully.

'I wish! I have a little money, but nowhere near what I'd need to buy somewhere like this, and no one is going to give an ex hotel housekeeper that kind of loan. But I can dream. Start small, work hard and, with a following wind and some luck, build up to something grander.'

'Jay! How are things? How is Chloe?' Sally said, swooping down on him before he could escape.

The awards evening had been a nightmare. Sally had been leaving him messages…

He'd had years of putting on a face, not letting his feelings show, smiling for the camera, but losing Chloe for a second time had been like forgetting how to breathe.

All he'd had from her was a brief text to let him know that she'd taken all her stuff from the flat, emptied the fridge, cleaned up but she hadn't said where she'd gone. Back to the horrible room he'd found her in, he had no doubt.

'I can't stop,' he said. 'I've got meetings.'

She caught his sleeve before he could dodge around her. 'Not so fast, Jay Harrington. Why have you been avoiding me?'

'I've been run off my feet since I got back from Paris.'

'Tell me about Paris.' She hooked an arm through his and steered him purposefully through the obstacle course of scaffolding, ladders and workmen to the quiet of a small alcove she'd temporarily commandeered for her drawing board. 'Where's Chloe? I assumed you'd bring her back with you.'

'She decided to stay in Paris.'

'As in permanently?'

'Yes.'

She muttered a profanity. 'I did warn you.'

'Don't blame Chloe. It was my fault. I messed up.'

'I find that hard to believe. You adore her and you're the sweetest, kindest man...' He gave a half-shake of his head. 'This has to be a mistake. What did you do?'

'She said I was behaving just like her father.'

'What? That's ridiculous.'

'Apparently not. And when you know everything that happened, you'll understand that there is no coming back from that.'

'Everything?' She took his hand. 'You look wrecked, Jay. Come around this evening.'

'I'm working—'

'It doesn't matter how late. I'm still running on Singapore time.'

'It suits you,' he said, finally looking at her. 'You have a sparkle.'

'And you look as if you haven't slept for days, but for all the wrong reasons.'

'Right first time, but there's nothing anyone can do about that.'

'I can listen.'

He managed a wry smile. 'Chloe told me that the world needs more people who know how to listen.'

'Did she?' She gave him a thoughtful look. 'That is interesting. Bring me something luscious from the restaurant and we'll see how that goes.'

'I'm not... I've passed the chef's hat to Freya. I've been working on a new project, one of the big hotels has asked if I'd be prepared to create a James Harrington afternoon-tea service, but something Chloe said is bothering me...' He shook his head. 'I need to talk to Hugo.'

'Don't we all!'

He gave her hand a reassuring squeeze. He had no confidence in her ability to help him with

Chloe, but there were things he needed to say to her.

'I'll be with you at about nine and I'll cook for us but right now I really need to find Hugo.'

'Tell him…' He waited, but she held up her hands, backing off. 'It's okay, I'll tell him myself.'

As Chloe walked up the stairs to the room where James had found her, her neighbour on the top floor passed her.

'Hi, Chloe, have you been away?'

'Just for a few days. Has there been a problem? The snow…?'

'No, but the landlord came around to check the pipes and when he didn't get an answer, he let himself into your place. When I caught him coming out, he made an excuse about checking your heating, but he's bound to have gone through your stuff.'

'There was nothing for him to find, but thanks for the warning.'

Marie had been glad to offer her a job and she'd stayed on at the château for a few days but, as she'd promised James, she had wasted no time in calling Julianne.

The woman had been all innocent sweetness and saying sorry that she wasn't coming back.

She unlocked the door. After nearly two weeks

shut up, it smelled of damp and, despite the cold, she dropped her bag, crossed to the window and threw it open. Then she saw the roses James had bought her.

The crisp white petals had softened and when she touched one of the flowers, they fell in a shower onto the table.

This was the moment to weep, but instead she felt a powerful surge of anger. Not with James, not even with her father.

With herself.

CHAPTER ELEVEN

'I'VE BROUGHT SCALLOPS,' Jay said, when Sally had buzzed him into her apartment.

'Fish? My neighbours will love you!'

'Sorry. I remembered how much you like them and, living above the restaurant, I don't have to think about food smells. If you've got some eggs, I'll make a soufflé omelette instead.'

'Help yourself, but just for you,' she said. 'I'm not hungry.'

He gave her a long look. 'Not hungry, or not eating?'

'Not hungry. Really,' she said when he didn't look convinced. 'Louis produced some wonderful veggie dish for us to taste at lunchtime, but to be honest my stomach doesn't know what time of the day it is.'

'If you need to sleep...'

'Oh, no,' she said, grabbing his arm as he made a move towards the door. 'You're not going anywhere until you've told me what happened in Paris. What would you like to drink?'

'If I'm going to face an inquisition it had better be Scotch with just a splash of water.'

'No inquisition.' She pushed him towards an armchair, poured a large measure of Scotch into a glass and handed it to him with a bottle of water, so that he could add his own. She topped up her own glass from a bottle of tonic water then curled up on the sofa. 'Okay. Start at the beginning and tell me everything.'

He took a sip of the Scotch, sat on the edge of the armchair. 'Can I get something off my chest first?'

'That sounds ominous.'

'No...' He looked into the glass he was holding. He'd planned what he was going to say, but this wasn't a moment for a speech. 'You said, when I saw you at the hotel, that I was the sweetest, kindest man.'

'You are.'

'No, Sally. No one sweet or kind would have walked out of school without a thought for you. Not caring how you would cope.'

'Jay...'

'You were struggling with the loss of Mum, afraid of Nick. I knew that and I abandoned you. I want you to know that I'm sorry I did that. To tell you that if you should ever need me again, I won't let you down.'

When he looked up, Sally was wiping a finger beneath her eye, blinking furiously.

'Oh, sorry, I've made you cry.'

'No… Yes…' She shook her head, laughing a little as she contradicted herself. 'I love that you felt the need to say that.' She reached across and laid a hand over his. 'I'm not denying that it was painful. You had always been there, a second heartbeat, and I felt desperately alone. And at the time I was angry… But you had just been hit with the kind of blow that would have broken many men and you were just a boy.'

'I grew up very quickly.'

'And look at you now,' she said.

'Now… Now I feel exactly like that boy, Sally. Confused, lost.' He swallowed a mouthful of whisky. 'The difference is that this time I'm going to have to live without hope.'

'There is always hope. Tell me what happened,' she urged softly.

For a while the only sound was the faint buzz of traffic, then Jay began talking. Starting at the beginning, the moment he'd seen Chloe's reflection in the window. Each step until he was at her door and that first extraordinary, clothes-tearing sexual meltdown…

'Wow…' Sally said, pulling at her collar to let in a little air. 'Just wow.'

'I mistook it for more than it was. I thought

she felt the same reconnection, the same till-death-us-do-part, second-chance joy.'

'I'm not sure that sex is ever that important.' He looked up and caught a look on her face. 'It sounds more as if you were both breaking a ten-year-long drought,' she continued briskly when she saw him watching her. 'Go on.'

He took the little leather folder from the pocket in his shirt, opened it and handed it to his sister. She looked at it, looked at him. 'Is this what I think it is? Chloe had the baby?'

'A girl. Chloe called her Eloise.'

'Oh, Jay...' She ran a hand lightly over the images then looked up, tears in her eyes. 'You have a little girl. I have a niece...'

'Yes, but the chances of us ever meeting are minimal. Chloe was forced to sign adoption papers.'

A hand flew to her mouth. 'She must have been heartbroken. How could they do that to her?' she said. 'Who cares about such things these days?'

'Thomas Forbes Scott cared. He had other plans for Chloe.' He told her the whole story. Their flight from her apartment...

'Why didn't you bring her straight back to London?'

'She flat out refused. I thought that she needed time to get her head around what had happened.'

Sally pulled a face.

'What?'

'A wee bit patronising.'

'Patronising?'

'You didn't need time,' she said. 'Ten minutes after incredible make-up sex, you were behaving like an alpha caveman. All that was missing was the club.'

'It wasn't like that,' he protested. 'I was happy to give her all the time in the world, but whenever I brought up moving to London, the future, she…' He shrugged.

Sally raised an eyebrow.

'She distracted me.'

'She wanted the sex but not the commitment?'

'She said she loved me, Sally.' He dragged a hand through his hair. 'I accepted her reasons for not wanting to go to the awards ceremony, but if she'd come home with me, there was time to book the registrar. We could have been married by Christmas.'

'Christmas! Are you completely mad? A woman wants more than a quick walk-through at the register office on one of the biggest days in her life.'

'It was just a formality. I said she could have the big-dress day later. At the château. Anywhere she chose.'

'*You* said. I'm getting a lot of what you said, Jay. What did Chloe say?'

'She said that she wasn't sure the château would still be in business. That she was worried about Marie. The woman who owns it.'

'Classic deflection technique. But what was the big hurry?'

'Chloe's father had shut her up in a private clinic once before. She had some kind of breakdown after they took the baby from her.'

'I'm not surprised, but what's that have to do with anything?'

'She's the heiress to a huge fortune living in a ghastly walk-up, taking minimum-wage jobs. Her father would have had no trouble finding doctors willing to swear that she was behaving irrationally, that she needed protecting from herself.'

'I'm surprised he hadn't already gone there.'

'Maybe he thought that eventually she would come to her senses. Accept the marriage he'd arranged. If she was married to me—to anyone—he would lose that control and he would try to stop it.'

'Did you tell her that?'

'I told her that I loved her, that I only wanted the best for her, that I just wanted to take care of her, protect her…' He got up, helped himself to another Scotch, drank it down in one mouthful.

'That's when she informed me that they were the words her father used when he was taking her from school, taking away our baby to give to strangers. When he was shutting her away in a clinic.'

'And what did you say?'

'She compared me to her father, Sally!'

'What did you say?' she repeated.

'That she had unresolved issues and that until she dealt with them, she would never have a life or a future.' Angry, hurt, he'd said worse. A lot worse...

Sally got up, took the bottle from his hand before he could pour another drink and put her arms around him.

'What should I have said, Sal?'

'Nothing.'

He looked at her. 'Nothing?'

'Nothing is always the best option when the alternative involves a very large foot in a wide-open mouth. Even if what you said is, I suspect, true.' She led him through to the kitchen and put on the kettle.

'You think I'm right?'

'Yes, but unfortunately being right is sometimes worse than being wrong. Always worse than just keeping quiet.'

She opened a cupboard, found a packet of camomile teabags and dropped one into a mug.

'I had such plans. I was talking to her about the tea service one of the big hotels wants me to set up for them. She had some great ideas. She even said that I needed to talk to Hugo first…'

'Hugo?'

'He'd said he had no problems with me setting up in a rival hotel, but she thought he was backing off to keep me happy. I wanted her to run it for me, Sally.'

'How did she feel about that?'

He thought about it. 'As I said, she was full of ideas,' he said. 'I thought she was eager to be part of it.'

'You thought?'

'Assumed,' he admitted.

'But you didn't ask her?'

'I didn't think I had to. I'd found her. We were going to get married. I even bought a big old mirror she liked.' His sister raised an eyebrow. 'She said that if she'd had a mantelpiece, she would have bought it.'

'And you were going to buy a house and give her the mantelpiece.'

'What's wrong with that?'

She rubbed a hand against his sleeve. 'You were full of plans for the future and you told her what her part was going to be in them.'

'I love her, Sally. I wanted her to see herself as part of my life. To be involved.'

'And what did she say?'

'It was getting late. She was hungry...' He shrugged. 'She said that talking about business gave her indigestion.'

She sighed. 'It must be a man thing.'

'What?'

'Not listening.'

'She fudged, Sally. She didn't say no. Not until she accused me of being like her father.'

'You did rather jump in with both feet. You knew exactly what you wanted, James. She needed you to ask what she wanted and when you didn't, I imagine she felt cornered. The difference is that this time she was strong enough to stand and fight.'

'Fight? I'm not her enemy.'

'No. Just carried away by a rush of excitement, energy, joy.'

She poured water onto the teabag, dunked it for a moment, then handed him the mug.

'I hate camomile tea, Sally.'

'I know, but it will help you sleep and when you've slept, you will go back to France, find Chloe and, on your knees, ask her what she wants. And listen to her.'

'She might not want to see me. Not after what she said.'

'You have to show her that you heard her. That you're listening.'

'After what I said.'

'I didn't say it would be easy. One final warning. Before you go you need to ask yourself one question.'

He took a sip of the tea, pulled a face. 'Go on.'

'What will you do if her plans, her dreams, are different from yours?'

'He's here, Chloe. Are you ready?'

Maître Bernier, the lawyer son of Marie, looked anxious. A second lawyer, who had travelled to this meeting from London, said nothing.

'Yes,' she said, rising to her feet. 'I'm ready.'

He nodded to his secretary, who returned a few moments later. 'Monsieur Thomas Forbes Scott,' she announced.

Chloe dug newly gelled nails into her palms, breathing carefully, forcing herself to remain calm as her father walked into the room. Not to betray by so much as a blink the slightest emotion. Deeply grateful for the boardroom table that stood between them so that he shouldn't see her knees knocking.

For a long moment he said nothing, just looked at her, absorbing every detail of her appearance.

He still had the arrogant command that had inspired both awe and a desperate need to please him when she was a child. As a girl. And later, fear.

His hair was streaked with silver these days, but his eyes were as dark and compelling as ever.

She remained statue-still under his scrutiny. Her hair had been cut and was hanging in a smooth bob over the classic camel blazer, silk shirt, casual trousers—a mix of charity and high-street bargains put together with French chic with the help of Marie's daughter-in-law, who had advised that nothing should look new.

The shoes had been an extravagance; her father would not be fooled by cheap shoes, but they had been very gently distressed, as if they were old and treasured friends.

The precious amber beads that had once belonged to her beloved maternal great-grandmother were the finishing touch. A message.

'Chloe,' he said, finally acknowledging her.

'Papa.'

'You asked for this meeting,' he said. 'Have you something to say to me?'

She had been thinking about what she'd say from the moment she'd asked for this meeting. There had been a hundred things. An entire essay of accusations to fling at him.

She wanted to look him in the face, challenge him to acknowledge the pain he had caused, but her father had studied law. A challenge invited a rebuttal and she would be forced to listen to him justifying every action with icy detachment.

They both knew what he'd done and if he had felt one jot of remorse, he would have sought her out long ago to beg her forgiveness.

She took a breath and, praying that her voice would not shake, she said, 'Maître Bernier, who is acting on my behalf, has obtained a copy of the will of Lady Alicia Gordon, my maternal great-grandmother. It appears that I inherited the bulk of her estate while a minor and which, as her executor, you have administered on my behalf.'

She managed to keep her voice even, level, despite the tremor beneath her ribcage. She was his daughter and she would show him how she had learned…

'Mr Peter Ward, who is a representative of Lady Alicia's solicitors, has come from London with documents for you to sign in order to release the estate to me.'

She indicated the documents lying on the table in front of him.

He didn't betray what he was thinking by so much as a flicker of an eyelash. No hint of regret that this meeting was not to be her surrender. Nor did he look at the papers.

'It was a very small estate but a great deal of money to be given to an unstable young woman. What do you intend to do with it?' he demanded.

'Play the tables at Monte Carlo?' she suggested. 'Or I might give it to a donkey sanctuary. Great-Grandma was very fond of donkeys.'

There was the slightest tightening of the muscles around her father's mouth as she baited him for lying to the lawyers about her mental health. It was only through Maître Bernier's careful diligence that she had discovered her inheritance. Her great-grandmother's solicitors had been astonished to learn that she had been living and working in Paris for years rather than confined to a clinic.

'Alternatively,' she said, 'I could hire a detective to discover the whereabouts of the baby you took from me in what Maître Bernier informs me was an illegal adoption.'

'You will never find her.'

The distinguished London solicitor, a man who had struggled to contain a smile at the mention of the donkey sanctuary, let slip a shocked breath.

'Are you sure, Papa? I have this photograph of her as a baby,' she said, sliding an enlarged picture of her holding the newborn Eloise from beneath the pile of documents. 'The hunt for the stolen Forbes Scott baby would be a sensation on social media and if I put it beside a photograph of me at the age she is now it's quite possible that someone will recognise her.'

'You would not do that.'

There wasn't a hint of uncertainty in that declaration; it was like fencing with a brick wall. But while it was true that she would never expose her daughter to the inevitable Internet frenzy, she had to protect her friends, Georges Bernier, herself, from any chance of retaliation for this day's work.

'I would,' she said, with equal conviction, 'should circumstances force me to it.'

She laid out the stark warning, holding those dark eyes for a long moment. His reputation, his status, his name, were everything to him and he had to believe the threat was real.

She'd thought it would be hard, but there was nothing left that he could do to hurt her. He finally recognised that too and when he looked away, she said, 'I think we're done here, Maître Bernier. Do you have a pen?'

Her father glared at him and then, as the Maître's secretary was hurriedly summoned to witness his signature, he produced the fountain pen he always carried with him from his inside jacket pocket.

He signed, the secretary signed and, when it was done, her father replaced the cap on his pen, returned it to his pocket and walked out of the office without a word to any of them.

There was a moment of awkward silence, then Mr Ward gathered up the papers, assuring her that the transfer of funds would be made within days.

'If you need any further assistance in anything that has arisen today, Miss Forbes Scott, we will be happy to assist.' Then, having shaken their hands, he left to catch his train back to London.

'You were magnificent, Chloe,' Georges Bernier said.

'I thought I would be terrified, but he was smaller than I remembered.'

'It is often the way with ogres. We build them up in our mind but, when we confront them, they are like the wizard in that old American movie.'

'Oz,' she said.

'Pardon?'

'The Wizard of Oz was all smoke and mirrors, Georges. My father is a lot more dangerous than that.'

'That is why you threatened to destroy his reputation?'

'He has intimidated people I love in the past and I wanted them, and you, to be safe.' Her one regret was that James had not been there to see him vanquished. To see her being strong... 'His name is the one thing he values.'

'Do you ever see your mother?' he asked as he saw her to the door.

'No.' She sagged a little. 'I hoped she might have come with him today. Seen me face him.'

'It's almost impossible for women to break free of controlling men, Chloe.'

'It happened to the mother of a friend of mine,' she said, thinking of James. 'The father of my baby.'

They had only been together for just under a week, but his absence was like the ache of a missing limb.

'Maybe, when your child is older,' he said, opening the door for her, 'she will search for you. And maybe, one day, your mother will find her own courage. It has to come from within.'

'But you need someone at your back.' Someone like James. 'Someone to show you the way.'

Georges took her red coat from the stand, held it for her.

'I'll be in touch when everything has been settled.' He gave her a long look as she dealt with the buttons. 'You *were* joking about Monte Carlo?'

'Yes, Georges. I was joking.' Then she grinned. 'But I quite like the idea of a donkey. Do you think Marie would mind?'

'A donkey would help keep the grass down in the paddock, but it will need a friend. Donkeys get lonely.'

'Do they?'

Why did she question that? Everyone got lonely…

'Two donkeys, then. And on the way home I am going to stop at Pierre Hermé and treat myself to raspberry and cream *macarons* to have with my coffee.'

Half an hour later she was climbing the stairs to her grotty little apartment when, as she neared the top, she found herself confronted by a pair of feet, crossed at the ankles and encased in a pair of familiar shoes.

'James…' He was sitting on the top step, blocking the way to her door. 'How was the awards evening?' she asked, since he appeared to have lost the ability to speak.

'Not great,' he admitted. 'My body was there. My heart was here. It made breathing tricky. If it hadn't been for Hugo, I'm not sure I'd have got through it.' He sighed. 'Sorry. I promised myself I wouldn't be pathetic.'

He got to his feet, moved to one side while she unlocked the door but waited for an invitation before he stepped inside.

'Don't stand in the doorway letting in the cold,' she said, aware how this had gone last time. How easily it could go the same way again, because she had been thinking about him as she'd bought the *macarons*. As she'd travelled back across Paris. Thinking about calling him, to tell him that he had been right. That because of him she had faced her demon and she was free.

But she had compared him to that demon, to the man he'd called a monster, and, like the words he'd used to hurt her, it contained a grain of truth.

'And I'll forgive the pathetic if you put on the kettle,' she said as she took off her coat. Keeping it snippy so that even if she was tempted to fling her arms around him, he would get the *Back off* message. 'Make a cup of tea and I'll share my *macarons*.'

'Pierre Hermé,' he said as she put the little carrier on the table and went to hang up her coat.

'A little treat,' she said. 'I was thinking of you earlier and how you used to sneak out of school and go to Covent Garden to buy them for me.'

'A visit to their café in the rue Bonaparte was on my list of things to do.'

'I'd have liked that,' she said. 'But we did a lot.'

'Yes…' He frowned. 'Have you got a new job?'

'I haven't got any kind of job at the moment,' she said. 'Thanks to you I am between jobs. Temporarily unemployed—'

'I'm sure your agency would find you something,' he said, a definite edge to his voice.

'The pathetic act didn't last very long.'

He shrugged. 'I have many faults, Chloe, but I keep my promises. Even the ridiculous ones I make to myself.'

'Yes, James.' She was forced to swallow down the lump in her throat. 'You always did. But you're right. I have no regrets about working in housekeeping but it's time to move on.'

'If you've been for an interview, I guarantee you've smashed it. You look amazing. As if you could take on the world.'

'Not an interview. And the look I was aiming for was chic Parisienne heiress with nothing to do but have lunch with her friends. But I'll take amazing.'

'Can I ask why?'

'Why are you here, James?'

He held up his hand. 'Sorry. You're right. It's none of my business what you do,' he said. 'I won't take a minute of your time. I just came to give you something.'

The vase he'd bought her, and which had still been in his car, along with their other purchases at the *brocante* when he'd left? Or the flamingo? Surely he wouldn't have returned to Paris to bring her a Christmas tree ornament?

'A courier would have been a lot cheaper than a ticket on the Eurostar.'

'The cost was not an issue. I came to give it to you in person so that I could apologise for being so dense. For not listening. For making you feel so bad that you compared me to your father.' He lifted his shoulders in an oddly awkward shrug.

'And I wasn't sure if you would still be here.' He looked around at the boxes, packed and waiting to be moved. 'It looks as if I'm only just in time.'

'I'm not running away, James. Not hiding. Not from you. Not from anyone. I was going to let you know where I'll be. And also, to apologise. What I said to you was unforgivable.'

She wanted to go to him, put her arms around him, lay her head against his shoulder and beg him to forgive her, but he was holding himself at a distance. No doubt protecting himself from being hurt for a third time.

There was also the risk that, having once put her arms around him, she would not let go. And she had plans of her own.

'I won't deny that it was like a knife to the gut,' he said, 'but I understand why you said it. Finding you was like having the lights switched back on but even while you were in my arms you were somehow out of reach. It wasn't so much that I didn't listen to you,' he said. 'It was that I didn't want to hear what you were saying.'

'In your arms was the one place I was totally with you, James. There was nothing held back. Nothing that wasn't true.'

CHAPTER TWELVE

THERE WAS A moment when she thought he might have taken a step towards her, but instead he unzipped his backpack, took out a velvet-covered box and put it on the table beside her.

Definitely not the vase and far too fancy for a Christmas tree ornament.

She picked it up, ran her fingers over the silky surface, looked up at him, frowned. 'What is this?'

'A memento of a simpler time.'

'My hairpin…' she said as she opened the box to reveal the silver pin lying in a satin nest.

It had been restored, not just the damage where he'd crushed it with his foot, but all the little dinks and knocks of the years she'd worn it had been smoothed out and polished so that it looked like new.

'Thank you, James. This was, is, very precious to me,' she said, running a fingertip along the curves, around the heart at its centre, just as she had when she'd first seen it all those years ago. 'I will take more care of it in future.'

'No…'

She looked up.

'Don't put it away in its box, Chloe. You might lose it again, or damage it, but it's like life. Not to be kept for best, but to be worn every day.' He picked up his backpack and slung it over his shoulder. 'That's it. What I came for. I'll leave you to enjoy whatever life that outfit is taking you to.'

'Wait…!' He was half turned from her so that she only had his profile. 'You came from London just to give me this?'

'It's just a couple of hours on the train and I didn't want our relationship to end on harsh words.'

'It will never end, James. We have a daughter. We might never find her, never be there for the great moments in her life, but because of her we are joined for ever.'

She saw him swallow, momentarily unable to speak, and she took a step towards him.

'It's her birthday at the end of January. Maybe I could come over to London and we could have lunch together? Raise a glass in celebration of her life.'

'London? You'd come to London for the day?'

She smiled. 'It's just a couple of hours on the train.'

'Touché.'

'I'm not scoring points. I told you, James, I'm

not running and I'm not hiding, and I have you to thank for that. You were absolutely right when you said my father was still controlling my life. Because of you I realised that I had to face him, or I would never be free. And now I have.'

Now she had his full attention. 'You've seen him?' he demanded. 'When?'

'This morning. Hence the disguise,' she said, indicating the outfit she was wearing. 'I had my hair trimmed and styled, my nails gelled, and I wore the amber necklace left to me by my great-grand-mother,' she said, fingering the big round beads that lay next to her throat, 'because he'd recognise it and he'd know that, however low he imagined I'd sunk, I had never been reduced to selling it.'

'I should have been there…' he began, then caught himself, holding up his hands in a gesture of surrender. 'I get it. It was something you had to do on your own.'

'Who are you?' she said, laughing. 'And what have you done with the real James Harrington?'

And, finally, he was grinning, too. 'Okay, you've got me. How did it go?'

'Let me buy you lunch,' she said, 'and I'll tell you.'

Somewhere, out in the city, over the sound of traffic a bell was sounding the Angelus. A door slammed below them. And Jay hesitated.

His intention in coming back to Paris had been an attempt to take their relationship back to the moment in the doorway when they'd both lost it and start again. Only this time do it right. Take nothing for granted.

Wait to be invited in but accept Chloe's decision if she chose to keep him on the doorstep.

Give her the repaired pin. Accept her decision if she didn't want it.

Apologise for not hearing her. Listen to what she said in response.

With each step he would leave the next move to her.

No touching, no hanging around waiting for more than she was prepared to give.

They had been skating on the surface of the past with him attempting to drag her into a future that he had planned. If they were to have a future, they needed to build something new. Together.

The offer of lunch was unexpected. But it was on her terms and if he had to bite his tongue to stop himself from insisting on paying for it, then that was what he'd do.

'How are your plans going?' Chloe asked as they walked down the road.

His plans were unimportant. Pretty much non-existent, if he was honest. He wanted to hear about the meeting with her father, but he curbed his curiosity.

'The book is with my editor,' he said, 'and a kitchen has been booked for a photographic session. I'm not looking forward to that.'

'And the tea service?'

'The hotel I was in talks with are not interested in the vintage theme.'

'It was only an idea, James.'

'I know, but it's one that I like too much to compromise on. It may fit the Harrington image, but Hugo and Sally appear to be at loggerheads over some design issue at the moment. It's not the moment to toss in another complication.'

He took her arm without thinking as they crossed the road. She didn't pull away but, remembering her comment about the elderly aunt with the walking stick, he let go as soon as they reached the other side.

'I always felt bad about the way I abandoned Sally when I walked out of school,' he told her, 'but we've talked. It's good.'

'Maybe I'll get a chance to see her when I come to London. How is your friend Louis settling in? It's a big change for him.'

'He's loving the creative freedom and producing some amazing food. The Harrington restaurant will have a star in no time.'

'That's great. No star here,' she said as they

reached a busy bistro. Despite the cold there were people sitting outside, drinking coffee and smoking. Inside it was warm and, as they waited for someone to spot them and seat them, Chloe was enveloped in a hug.

'*Chérie!* It's so good to see you! Have you changed your mind?'

'Sorry, Augustin, I'm just here for lunch with my friend from England.'

'England?' Augustin gave him a long look. 'Your face is familiar, *monsieur.*'

'James is a chef, Augustin. His restaurant has a Michelin star. He's a bit of celebrity but he loves honest French cooking. So, do you have a quiet table for us?'

'That depends, darling girl, on whether or not he is the reason I found you in tears the last time you were here.'

The clink of cutlery on dishes, the lively hum of conversation, dimmed as Jay turned to look at Chloe.

'Tears?'

'I had just discovered that I'd lost my hairpin,' she said, taking his hand before turning to Augustin. 'The silver one that your wife admired so much? James found it, bent and broken. He's had it repaired and has travelled from London today for the sole reason of returning it to me. I wanted to buy him lunch to thank him and where else would I bring him?'

The man melted, made a slight bow in his direction and a few moments later they were seated in a quiet corner. Menus were produced but Jay shook his head.

'I am in your hands, Augustin.'

Wine arrived. White, and crisp as a winter morning. Water. Warm bread, fresh from the oven. Butter from Normandy. A wonderful vegetable broth…

'This is the way to live,' he said. 'Everyone relaxed, focussed on the good food Augustin has placed in front of them.'

'He would be flattered to hear you say that.'

'It's not flattery,' he said. 'It's the truth. In London lunch is something to be grabbed on the run. Traders come into the ground-floor bar and are never off their phones. I doubt they even taste the food.'

'That's terrible, but it must be different upstairs?' she said. 'I've seen the photographs on the website. Your dining room is so elegant, and the food looks just beautiful.'

'Fine food for people who are counting every calorie. Pictures for their social-media pages to show the world that they are living an aspirational lifestyle. Businessmen and women whose only interest is the deal they're making.'

He heard the words he was saying and didn't know where they'd come from.

'You sound a little disillusioned.'

'Am I being ungrateful?' he asked.

'Honest, maybe.'

'It's not all like that. In the evening there are family parties, celebrations, couples getting to know one another. The occasional proposal, choreographed with the help of my staff.'

'That must be fun.'

'Yes, it is. The best part, but an occasional proposal is not enough. I seem to have reached a peak, Chloe. Fulfilled all those early ambitions I bored you with when we were at school. I'm not yet thirty and suddenly I'm wondering where do I go from here?'

'Another star?' she suggested, and there had been a time when that had seemed important, but he shook his head. 'Is that what the tea-service idea is about? A new challenge?'

'I suppose so, but, put like that, it seems like a very small ambition.' He managed a smile. 'First-world problems, Chloe,' he said, shaking it off. He wasn't there to talk about him. He was in Paris to listen to Chloe. 'Tell me about your meeting with your father. How did you set it up?'

'After you left, Marie insisted I stay the night with her. While I was there Claud, her chef, phoned to tell her that his wife had broken her hip in the fall. She's not young, it's going to be a long job.'

'Poor woman.'

'It's not good. Marie is fairly certain that even if she recovers fully, she'll decide not to return to work. In the meantime, Claud is spending all his time at the hospital and when she comes home, he'll be needed to take care of her.'

'Will they manage?' he asked, concerned.

She nodded. 'They don't have to work. They both have good pensions, but they enjoyed working at the château because it was not full time. It was Marie who was in a fix. She had a full house that weekend for a Christmas craft workshop being run by a television celebrity.'

He grinned. 'And of course, you offered to help.'

'I was happy to stay for the weekend and pitch in.'

'Happy, full stop,' he said. 'I saw your face when we drove through the gates of the château and I know what love at first sight looks like. I take it she's offered you a job?'

'I'd already asked her if she'd take me on as an intern. I wanted to learn about the events business.' She nodded. 'I just came back to Paris to pack up.'

'And to meet with your father.'

'Yes, that.'

Chloe smiled up at Augustin, who had paused at a discreet distance to check whether they needed anything. Whether the food was to their liking.

He would have given it five stars no matter what it tasted like, but it was excellent and, curbing his impatience to hear Chloe's story, he said so and received a compliment on his French in return.

They ate while the soup was still hot but when the plates were cleared Chloe said, 'I told you that meeting you again was a moment I'd dreamed about, James. And it was a dream. But my first instinct was to run, disappear...'

She paused but he didn't leap in to reassure her, tell her that he understood. A passing waitress topped up their water glasses.

'It was wonderful being together,' she said, once they were alone, 'but while you were offering me your life, I was still running away.'

'Because you want your own life,' he said. 'It took me a while. A verbal slap around the head from Sally, but you deserve to be so much more than an add-on to mine.'

The one he'd thought so perfect until he was faced with living the rest of it without Chloe.

'That is true,' she said, 'but being with you showed me that I had no life at all. When I left home, when I began running away, I didn't imagine I'd still be living like this years later.'

She paused and smiled up at Augustin as he placed a simple chicken casserole before them, listed the ingredients, then said a brief, *'Bon appetit!'* and left them to their meal.

'Not like this,' Chloe said, with a smile, as she turned her hand to indicate the table in front of them.

'I know.'

'You were right when you said that my father was controlling my life and I'm not denying that it was a shock, painful to hear, but that didn't make it any less true. If I was Sleeping Beauty, your kiss was a lot more than a wake-up call.'

'It was a lot more than a kiss,' he said.

'It was and I loved every minute of it.' And her smile was a lot more than going through the motions. It reached out, warming him as if she'd got up and put her arms around him.

'Marie's son is a lawyer and, once I'd decided that I had to face my father, I asked him if he'd be prepared to contact my father and set up a meeting in his office.' She took a sip of water. 'I did warn him that he'd be making an enemy.'

'But he agreed. Brave man.'

'Yes. He's been amazing.'

He heard the warmth in her voice and discovered that he possessed a hitherto undisturbed streak of jealousy.

'How did that go?' he asked. 'Did you get a grovelling apology? Did he go down on his knees begging for forgiveness?' he asked, hating that he sounded so cynical.

The man was Chloe's father and, no matter what he'd done, nothing could ever change that.

'What do you think?' she asked.

'You know what I think, Chloe. I'd have gone after him myself when you told me what he'd done but his lawyers would have shut me down in a heartbeat. All it would have done was expose you.'

'My hero.' She reached across the table. Briefly laid her hand over his. Her touch went through him like a charge of electricity and, as if she felt it too, she quickly removed it to push back a strand of hair that hadn't moved.

'No hero,' he said. 'And no begging, I'm guessing.'

'He said my name. I acknowledged him in return and then he asked me if I had anything to say to him. Clearly he thought I was the one who was going to be on my knees pleading to be allowed to return to the family fold.' She managed a shaky little laugh. 'I have to admit the knees were a bit wobbly.'

'But they did not bend.'

'No.' She pulled a face. 'Like it or not, James, I'm his daughter. The genes cannot be denied.'

'You have his strength, Chloe. Something I failed to understand and for that I'm sorry. But you don't have his weakness.'

She frowned. 'Weakness?'

'His pride, his arrogant belief that he is superior to the rest of us mere mortals. His vanity.'

'Oh.' She sat back in her chair. 'But that is what gives him his power.'

'It's not a power that I would want.'

'No.' His pride had denied him the joy of a granddaughter. She very much doubted the earl-in-waiting would have allowed the inconvenience of a love child to stand between him and a handsome dowry, should she have been prepared to knuckle under and marry him. Everyone had mix-and-match families these days.

'What happened, Chloe? What did he say? What did you say?'

'Um… Not much. But you can rest assured that there no longer exists any risk to you or any member of your family. Or to me.'

He stared at her for a moment. 'You threatened him?'

'Yes. Georges was right after all. He was like the Wizard of Oz, all smoke and mirrors. I hadn't realised it, but I always held the power.'

'Chloe? What did you do?'

'I looked him in the eyes, James, and offered him a choice. On the one hand public exposure, disgrace, his name dragged through the mud for conspiring in an illegal adoption to hide his own granddaughter. On the other, his assurance that everyone I know and love will live free from his malice.'

He let slip an expletive.

'What did he say?'

'Nothing. But he looked away first.'

'That was it?'

'There was a document for him to sign, family business, nothing to do with any of this. When he'd done that he left.'

'Without another word?'

'There was nothing left to say.'

'I guess not.' Then, 'Who's Georges?'

'Georges Bernier. Marie's son.'

'The brave lawyer.'

'Yes.' She smiled as if she knew what he was thinking. 'It was his very chic wife who helped me to put this outfit together.'

'I'm glad you had people to help you,' he said. 'And tomorrow you'll be moving to the château to start a new life?'

She nodded. They ate their lunch, declined a dessert. And Jay sat on his hands while Chloe paid.

Outside, a light flurry of snow caught them

and he hailed a taxi, but when he opened the door for her she said, 'You take it, James. I can walk.'

'And get wet. I've plenty of time so why don't I take the cab and ask the driver to drive me to the Gard du Nord via your apartment?'

It was a short ride to the apartment but, when the car stopped outside her building, she made no move to leave.

'Thank you for today, James.'

'As I recall, you paid for lunch. I should be thanking you.'

'Lunch was really nice, but I meant thank you for having my pin repaired. For taking the trouble to bring it back to me.'

'Did you think I'd throw it in the bin?'

'Most men would have done, but then you are not most men.' She looked across at him. 'Take care of yourself, James.' He made a careless gesture and she caught his hand. 'No. I mean it. I'm concerned about you.'

'There's a switch,' he said, but Chloe not only looked fabulous, there was a real change in her.

His instinct to protect her had not been wrong. All the time that she'd been with him, she had been mentally looking over her shoulder.

Now she was looking forward and she credited him with helping her to do that, which gave him hope that they could, maybe, find their way to a future together.

The taxi driver, who was paid less when he was moving slowly or at a standstill, held up his wrist and pointed at his watch.

He promised him extra to cover the time and then turned back to Chloe. 'Do you realise that we've never dated?'

'You have to go, James. You'll miss your train.'

'There'll always be another train,' he said, but there would never be another Chloe.

'We've spent a lot of time together, had a lot of sex, had a baby, but we've never done that thing where a guy calls for a girl, takes her out and then, at the end of the evening, walks her back to her front door and if he's lucky gets a kiss goodnight.'

'Do people do that any more?'

'I have no idea, but I think they should.' She was still holding his hand. 'If I come to Paris, can we do this again? Just have lunch while you tell me what you're doing?'

'But I won't be here, James. I'll be at the château.'

A caveat, but she hadn't said no.

'I can come and pick you up.'

'You'd do that?' she asked, but she was smiling. 'Okay. Let me know when you're coming and if it doesn't clash with an event at the château it would be lovely to see you. But you don't have to drive all the way out to Thoiry. I could meet you in Paris…'

'I'm afraid the dating rules state that I have to pick you up from your home and return you safely to your door.'

'The front door or the bedroom door?'

'The dating rules are clear on that, too. No sex before the third date. And only then if all parties think it would be fun.'

'Oh, I know it would be fun.'

'Maybe we need to concentrate on the things that we don't know, Chloe.'

'James…'

'I think we've tried this man's patience long enough,' he said, because leaving her while she still had something to say seemed like a smart idea.

Doubts, he didn't want to hear.

Questions, on the other hand, meant she would be all the more eager to meet him when he called.

Still holding her hand, he climbed from the back of the taxi and when she was standing on the pavement beside him, he lifted it briefly to his lips.

'I'll call you.'

Chloe remained on the footpath watching the taxi until it disappeared around the bend, stepping sideways to catch the last sight of James, hoping that he might look back. Not entirely sure what had just happened. Only that she was both happy and confused and a little bit afraid.

She was happy that James had taken so much trouble to bring back her hairpin. She was very happy that they were friends.

Was she happy that he wanted to see her again? That was confusing because it had to be pretty stupid on both counts. They both knew there was no future for her and James when their lives were in different countries.

And she was a little bit afraid because, although she knew how thorny this could get, how great the possibility of hurt for either or both of them, right at that moment she didn't care.

All she cared about was how soon it would be before he called her.

CHAPTER THIRTEEN

'HOW DID IT GO, JAY?'

He'd seen the missed call and picked up Sally's voicemail as he walked from the underground to L'Étranger and she rang again while he still had the phone in his hand.

'Hi, Sal. I was on the Tube when you rang. I was going to call you as soon as I got home.'

'Well?' she demanded. 'What happened?'

'I gave her the hairpin. Kept my distance. Listened more than I spoke but Chloe had just seen off her father and she asked me to lunch so that she could tell me what happened.'

'Lunch? Were you not listening? The plan was for you to stay for no longer than ten minutes!'

'The first casualty of any battle is the plan, Sally.'

'Really? I despair!'

'Don't do that. Chloe was bubbling. She needed to talk to someone who didn't need explanations. Someone who knew how important that meeting was.'

'Okay. We can recover from this. What happened?'

'Chloe took me to the bistro where she used to work, defended me to her ex-boss, who was ready to do me serious harm because he thought I'd made her cry, and, when she insisted on paying for lunch, I managed to restrain the macho urge to snatch the bill from her hand.'

Sally laughed. 'I'd have paid good money to see that.'

'This is the new, listening James Harrington.'

'Just listening? How close did you get?'

'Opposite sides of the table, I swear. No footsy.'

'Did you kiss?'

'Only her hand.'

'Ooh…'

'Was that wrong?'

'How could that ever be wrong? I'm melting at the thought of it. How did you leave things?'

'That we should try dating for a while.'

'Dating?'

'Lunch, cinema, ice skating. "Holding hands in the old-fashioned way" dating.'

'Sweet.'

'Don't mock,' he said, dodging around a group of girls blocking the path.

'I'm not. I wish I'd thought of it. It's brilliant.'

'But complicated by the fact that Chloe is

moving out of the vile flat to go and work for Marie Bernier at the château.'

'I don't blame her. I looked at it online and immediately wanted to spend a night or two there myself.'

'No reason why you shouldn't. You could mix business with pleasure and run an interior-design weekend course there.'

'You could cut down on the travelling and offer a cordon bleu cookery masterclass,' she suggested. 'Maybe one of your television contacts would like to film it?'

'Nice thought but I've just got to the restaurant, Sally. We'll talk soon.'

He disconnected, slipped the phone into his pocket and, instead of using the side entrance that led directly up to his apartment, he walked through the front door of L'Étranger.

The place was buzzing as the early evening traffic began to build up.

He'd only handed over the kitchen to Freya a couple of weeks earlier, but already he could feel a subtle change. Nothing anyone else would notice. Nothing he could put his finger on.

He spoke to members of staff as he walked through the ground-floor bar. Stopped to talk to customers who knew him, congratulating those who were there to celebrate some special occasion.

He thought about going into the kitchen, but it was Freya's domain now. The job of an executive chef was to advise, to plan for future growth, to approve and direct. Not to turn up and get in the way when service was in full swing.

Upstairs, in his flat, he sat down in his arm-chair, still in his overcoat and scarf, and wondered how long he had to leave it before he called Chloe.

Sally would almost certainly say a week.

There wasn't a chance in hell that he could wait that long, but when he checked his calendar on his phone, he discovered that there was something every day into the distance.

Hugo had some legal stuff he wanted to clear with him. He was booked to be a guest chef on a cookery show that was being filmed live on Saturday. His publisher's publicity people were desperate to tie up dates for interviews and a book tour. It had sounded like fun when he was signing the contract, but it would take a couple of weeks out of the spring when getting to France would be almost impossible. He went through it, trying to work out what was immovable and what he could shift…

Chloe's phone was ringing.

It had been five days. Five unbelievably busy days. The many strands of delivering an events package were a huge learning curve. There were bookings up to two years ahead that already involved putting details in place. Prompts in the diary at the point when menus, flowers, a dozen details needed to be actioned, confirmed, chased.

It had kept her mind occupied throughout the day and sometimes into a sleepless night, but always, in the background, every time her phone rang, she felt that dangerous little heart leap.

James had texted a sweet thank you for lunch. Sent her an animated 'good luck' card for the new job. The kind of thing you'd send a friend. Which was lovely.

She wanted them to be friends, always.

She wanted more but was always conscious of walking a tightrope between two incompatible dreams.

Mostly, though, she just hoped that it was him, but when she finally saw his name come up on the caller ID her hand was shaking as she answered and, suddenly stupidly shy, said, 'Hello, James.'

'Hello, Chloe. How did the move go? Are you settled in at the château?'

Normal, everyday questions. But then he'd had time to work out what he was going to say before he called.

'The move went as they always do,' she said. 'There was a certain amount of stress and disaster, but I'm here, nothing of any great value was broken and I'm learning a lot.'

'That's wonderful. Obviously you're not in one of the guest suites, but do you have a room with a view?' he asked.

Talk about a conversation with your maiden aunt!

'I'm on the top floor in a big room that is twice the size of my Paris flat with a view over the lake.'

'Does it have a mantelpiece?'

Okay, now it was getting weird. 'Yes. Is it important?'

'It could be. I had a sudden wild impulse to buy a big old gilt mirror at a *brocante*, recently. It's going to be picked up next week, but I don't actually have room for it. I was going to arrange storage but then I wondered if you had a handy mantelpiece where it might feel at home.'

'My mirror?' she asked. 'You bought my mirror?'

'And the armchair, but I have a home for that. So? Would you like it?'

'Yes, James…' She swallowed, took a breath. She would not cry… 'I would be very happy to save you the expense of storage.'

'That's very kind of you. I'll ask the driver to text you when he'll be arriving.'

Was that it? The reason for his call?

'Apart from an excess of furniture, how are you doing?' she asked.

'I'm good. Busy. Sally sends her love. She's fallen in love with the château, too. I suggested that she could run an interior design class there one weekend.'

'That's a wonderful idea. I'd love to see her. Tell her to give me a call and we can talk about it.' Then, because this conversation was setting up all kinds of tugs, both physical and emotional, and she was in danger of keeping him talking just to hear his voice, she said, 'I have to go, James.'

'Wait… Sorry, the mirror wasn't actually the reason for my call. I know it's ridiculously short notice, but someone just cancelled a meeting for tomorrow. Is there any chance that you'll be free? I'll completely understand if you have an event coming up this weekend and you're neck-deep in preparations. The job has to come first.'

'It does,' she agreed, 'but this weekend is clear, so we are not at panic stations. What did you have in mind?'

'A walk by the Seine if it's not raining. Lunch somewhere. Skating and hot chocolate, or maybe cocktails, at the Plaza Athénée?'

'I'll have enough trouble keeping on my feet with hot chocolate. And won't you be driving?'

'I thought I'd book a car with a driver,' he said.

'That way I'll be able to sit in the back and hold your hand. Maybe, after skating and cocktails, you'll fall asleep on my shoulder.'

'That is entirely possible,' she said, smiling at the thought.

'So? Is that a yes?'

Who was this James Harrington who took nothing for granted? Asked questions and listened to the answers?

'I would love to do all of that with you,' she said, 'but, James…'

'Chloe?'

'I want to be quite clear on one point.' He waited. 'Will this be our first or second date?'

He just laughed. 'Give my best to Marie,' he said, and then he was gone.

The two excitable French bulldogs, Beau and Felix, greeted him with unalloyed joy and a much more relaxed Marie with kisses on both cheeks.

'It makes me very happy to see you here, James.'

'Thank you, Marie. I hope Chloe feels the same way. How are things with you?'

'Perfect. Chloe…' She turned as she heard her on the stairs. 'Chloe is my angel.'

She was wearing a soft cream sweater, her gold curls fastened up in the silver pin.

'An angel?' He kissed her on both her cheeks with the same formality with which he'd greeted Marie, but drinking in the scent of her, holding it in his lungs. Desperately trying to block out what his life would be like if he could not see her.

She whirled around, laughing at his doubt. 'See my wings, baby. Watch me fly...'

It was true, he thought. She looked as if all it would take was a leap into the air and, like Peter Pan in a show his mother had taken them to see one Christmas when he and Sally were six years old, she would be flying around the room.

'Let's stick to the road for now,' he suggested as she tugged on her coat, wrapped a scarf around her neck. Unnerved by her joy.

What the hell did he think he was doing?

What would he do if Chloe had found her dream and there was no place in it for him?

'Sorry, guys,' he said, distracted by the dogs as they tried to follow Chloe into the car.

'Next time you must stay,' Marie said as she grabbed them by the collar, 'and take them for a walk.'

He was momentarily lost for an answer, his brain freewheeling, then catching as he realised that right now that was exactly what he wanted to do. But the driver had closed the door and, before he could think of a way to say that, the car was pulling away.

'The dogs like you,' Chloe said. 'Have you ever had one of your own?'

He shook his head. 'My mother was nervous around them and, although we didn't live in the hotel, the house was, is, in the grounds and my father was concerned about the guests.'

'The guests here don't mind them,' she said. 'I suspect your father was protecting your mother.'

'You may be right. I was only six when Dad died, but recent events have brought back so many memories. I can see now that while she was his light, had enormous charm, had enchanted the hotel guests, there was a fragility to her.' Had he absorbed that as a small child? Subconsciously recognised the way his father had protected her? Tried to do the same with Chloe? He looked at her, so confident, so strong… 'You are nothing like her,' he said. 'Apart from the light. It shines from you, too.'

She reached out her hand and found his. 'There was a moment when I could have broken. It was only the anger that kept me from going under all those years. It was anger that drove me to see my father.' Her hand tightened on his. 'I've been given a new life, James, and I have you to thank for that.'

'You did it for yourself.'

'But you were the catalyst.'

'I was cruel.'

'You said what you saw, and I wasn't angry with you. I was angry with myself. If you hadn't been so determined to find me, nothing would have changed.' She looked at him. 'I was so deep in the rut I'd worn for myself that I wasn't able to see over the top. See that there was another life out there.'

'Then I'm glad. I don't think I've ever seen you look so happy,' he said. 'Not even when we were young.'

'I'm having such a good time,' she said. 'The château, of course, but I'm able to use everything I know. Use the management skills and the financial acuity that I learned at my father's knee. That stood me in good stead while I've had to earn my own living. And Marie is teaching me about planning events. The details...'

She filled the journey to Paris with all that she'd done, learned, since he'd last seen her. Bubbling with an enthusiasm that he had once felt in the early days in the restaurant.

Envied.

He didn't have to ask what he'd do if Chloe's dream wasn't his. What he needed was a new dream that would live alongside hers.

They walked for a while, had a simple lunch, took to the ice in the beautiful courtyard of the Plaza Athénée, laughed a lot as they made idiots of themselves, drank hot chocolate and a final cocktail, before they climbed back into the car to be driven back to the château.

Chloe didn't fall asleep, but she leaned against him and he put his arm around her, holding her until they were home, and walked her up the steps to the door, where she turned to him.

'I don't want this to end, James.'

It was an invitation to stay, but he opened the door. 'Hold that thought.'

Marie appeared. 'Don't keep him on the doorstep, Chloe. Bring him in for coffee. I'm off to bed.'

It was a conspiracy, he thought, but, much as he wanted to stay, to wake up with Chloe beside him, he fought the temptation.

'Thanks, but it's going to be tight as it is to catch my train and I have a meeting first thing. But maybe next time I could talk to you about your wine, Marie?'

'Of course. It will be a pleasure.' She nodded, disappeared, leaving them to their goodbyes.

'Is there going to be a next time, Chloe?'

'You're afraid of being hurt.'

'Right now,' he said, 'I'm just afraid you'll decide that there's no future in this. No future for us.'

'Don't overthink it, James. Call me when you've got a spare day,' she said, 'and we'll enjoy what we have.' Then, almost as an afterthought,

'Just checking, here. Do the dating rules say that I'm allowed to call you?'

'Whenever you like,' he said. 'To talk, to arrange a date, or just so that I can listen while you breathe.'

'I'll do that,' she said, then leaned forward to kiss him lightly on the lips.

'Send me a text to let me know that you've got home safely.'

'James, is this a convenient time?'

He made an *I've got to take this* gesture and, as he walked in the corridor, said, 'It couldn't be more perfect.'

'You've just walked out of a meeting, haven't you?'

'I was in a meeting with my accountant so when I said it was the perfect moment, that was exactly what I meant.'

She laughed, but said, 'I'll keep it brief—'

'Don't! He's talking about some new accounting program.'

'Then listen to him. It's important.'

'I'd rather listen to you.'

'I've noticed, so listen. I called to let you know that the mirror has arrived, and I was wondering if you'd like to come and see how good it looks on my mantelpiece.'

Oh, the innocence in that voice. The temptation in that invitation.

He'd introduced the mirror into her bedroom so that she would think about him every time she looked in it, but his sneaky little ruse had just spectacularly backfired on him.

He knew she would be smiling at her cleverness, while he was leaning against the wall, catching his breath and trying desperately not to think about the silky skin of her breasts, the brief touch of her lips that had burned him up all the way back to London.

'We have date number two before we can even think about that,' he said, in an attempt at cool amusement, but there was no disguising the rasp of sexual desire in his voice. 'When were you thinking?'

'Tuesday or Wednesday?'

'Tuesday,' he said, without checking his calendar. Whatever was on it, he'd cancel. 'We can take the dogs for that walk. And I want to talk to Marie and her *vigneron* if that can be arranged,' he said, in an effort to restore the balance a little.

'I'll tell her.'

'It has been a most interesting day, Marie. Thank you.'

'I had no idea that you were so knowledgeable about viticulture, James.'

'I've been reading a lot about wine making in the last couple of weeks. Tasting with my own sommelier and the man my brother has taken on for the family hotel. They were both impressed with the character of your wine.'

'My husband hoped to achieve *grand cru*. He was close, but the first heart attack took the fire from his belly,' she said. 'But what is your new interest?'

'English winemakers are producing sparkling wines that, these days, are winning world-class medals.'

'You are considering planting a vineyard? In England?' she asked. 'It takes many years before you can harvest a vintage.' She lifted her hands. 'Don't waste your precious time talking to an old woman. Chloe wants to show you her part of the château.'

'*Madame...?*'

'Go, foolish boy. It's on the top floor. The third door on the left.'

He climbed the stairs, tapped on the door, opened it when Chloe called out for him to come in.

She was sitting at a little desk beneath the window, the dogs curled up at her feet. She had been working on her laptop and looked up as he entered.

'Did you enjoy your time with the *vigneron*?' she asked.

'Yes. I learned a lot.' He looked around the room, which had been prettily furnished. 'This is rather lovely. And the mirror looks as if it's been there for ever,' he said as she got up and joined him.

'And the little blue vase looks perfect next to it. I'd very much like to give you a thank-you kiss for that. Kisses are allowed on a second date, aren't they?'

'Chloe…' He wanted to hold her, kiss her, but he shook his head. 'I'm not sure I can handle this.'

'No more dates?' The little crack in her voice gave him hope.

'Being apart. We're not kids any more, and this isn't a game. I wanted to build something solid, from the ground up. I love you. What we have is the reason I draw breath…'

'James…'

'I know. You don't want London, or a tea room, or my life. But without you, all of that is meaningless.'

'But it was your dream, James. I can't take that from you.'

'If it was still my dream,' he said, 'I'd be there now, but something has changed at L'Étranger. I thought at first it was because Freya is now in charge of the kitchen, but it wasn't that. The only thing that has changed is me.' He swallowed down the boulder that was building in his throat. 'I have become the outsider in my own life.'

'Sweetheart…' She put her arms around him. 'How can I help?'

He clung to her. 'Just tell me what you want, Chloe, what you dream about when you're awake and the moon is shining in your window, and if I have to rattle the stars to make it happen, I'll give it to you.'

'This is my dream, James. The weddings, the events. I can see such possibilities. Even vintage English tea parties…'

'Don't tease. Just tell me that there's a place for me in that dream?'

She leaned back so that she could look at his face, look into his eyes. 'You're serious? You'd move to France?'

'I'd move to the moon if you were there. But I have to admit that France is a lot more attractive.'

'But what about your restaurant? Your book tour? Your television appearances? Your family? You can't just walk away.'

'I have already begun to. As executive chef at L'Étranger I remain the hand on the tiller, but Freya runs the restaurant. If she needs me, she can pick up the phone, or we can video call, and I can spend a day in London once or twice a month. It's only a couple of hours on the train, and I'd always be home by nightfall.'

Her smile emboldened him.

'There's nothing I can do about the book tour. I signed a contract and it will be an intense couple of weeks when getting home might not be possible, but I'll never go to sleep without calling you.'

'And television?'

'Sally suggested I might run some master-classes here.'

'And get a television company to film them?'

'She suggested it would be better to set up our own company, hire in the talent and sell the programmes we make to the networks. Cookery, craft, wedding planning…?'

She clapped a hand over her mouth. 'That is a genius idea! The possibilities are endless…'

She flung her arms around him and this time there was no holding back and her kiss had only one destination, but even as she was backing him towards the bed he broke away.

'Wait. Love…'

'Really? You're going to insist on waiting for a third date?'

'When we've talked to Marie, settled the deal, you can do whatever you want with me,' he promised.

'Oh,' she said, then added an uncharacteristic expletive.

'Oh?' He didn't like the sound of that 'oh' or what had followed. 'Oh, what?'

'You're too late. Marie has already found a buyer.'

'What?' He pulled away, dragged a hand through his hair. 'I'm so sorry. I'm such a fool. I've been playing at dating when I should have been—'

'No!' She put her arms around him. 'The dating has been lovely. Very frustrating, but right. We're different people from those desperate teenagers. We needed time…'

'We'll find somewhere else,' he promised. 'France is full of châteaux. When you fall in love with one, we'll make it our own dream.'

'No, James.'

'No…'

'This is awkward. I was going to wait until the third date to tell you that you were having breakfast in bed with the new chatelaine of Château St Fleury.'

It took him a moment.

'You? You've bought it? How?'

'The papers my father signed the day I met him were to release an inheritance from my great-grandmother. She died when I was seven and I didn't know about the bequest until Georges did some searches and turned it up. It wasn't a huge amount, but my father has been administering it and over nearly twenty years it had become quite substantial.'

'So that first day, when I came to give you your hairpin, you already knew you were going to buy it?'

'Are you annoyed with me for keeping it from you?'

He shook his head. 'On the contrary, I think you're the most amazing woman I've ever met. I just have one question.'

'Yes?' she asked.

'Will you give me a job?'

'How about I give you half the château?'

'I've got a better idea. Sell me the vineyard.'

'The vineyard?'

'I told you I needed something new and planting a vineyard in Sussex was my fall-back plan. A project to bury myself in if you decided that you didn't want me in your future.'

'Doesn't it take years to establish a vineyard?'

'I'd have had years.'

'And one day you would have been winning gold medals.' She lifted her hands to cup his face. 'I'm in need of a little cultivation myself, James Harrington. If I agree to sell you the vineyard,' she said, 'can we forget the damn third date and go to bed?'

EPILOGUE

SEAN STOOD BENEATH a canopy of spring blossoms and waited for his bride.

He and Fiona had done all the legal bits in a simple register office ceremony back home in Edinburgh, but this was their big day. The celebration of their marriage, with the fabulous dress, the flowers, the special, forever vows made in the company of their family and friends.

The grass had been cut, huge pots were overflowing with plants in the bride's chosen colour scheme.

Every pane of glass in the orangery had been polished. The tables were laid with white damask cloths, heavy silver, crystal glasses. The pastel napkins had been embroidered in the French style, with the name of each guest—a keepsake for them to take home.

The champagne was on ice, the château's finest vintage wines at a cool room temperature, the wedding breakfast created by a famous chef and waiting to be served by the army of helpers from the village for whom the château provided a little extra income.

A harpist played and as Fiona, looking serene and lovely in a simple cream lace dress, was walked down the aisle between the chairs on the arm of her kilted father, a young French baritone began to sing Robert Burns' 'My Love Is Like a Red Red Rose...'

It was Chloe and James's first wedding at the Château St Fleury, but Marie had remained on hand with advice, and the families were now close friends.

Chloe saw James take a breath as Fiona joined her new husband, remember to smile before addressing the gathering and then invite Sean to make his vows.

They were simple, heartfelt, and Chloe had to blink back a tear as she remembered the moment that she and James had sworn their own vows in the *mairie*.

He had encouraged her to reach out to her mother and invite her to the ceremony. He had been too young to understand about emotional coercion, the abusive mind control that Nick had exerted over his mother, and she was long beyond his help.

But he knew Chloe hoped that one day her own mother might break free and he wanted her to know that she had a refuge with them if she needed it.

Friends and family had gathered to witness their marriage. Marie and all her family. People who worked for James. Even his publisher had travelled from London. It was only after they had made their vows and had turned around to acknowledge the clapping that she had seen her mother standing at the back of the room. Older but still elegant and beautiful, and with tears pouring down her cheeks.

She would not stay for the party, but she had come. And she sent them postcards from wherever she was. And last week they had met in Paris.

Baby steps...

She smiled as James invited Sean to kiss his bride and then it was non-stop with lunch in the orangery, dancing on the terrace, children playing games organised by a professional nanny. Tea... And then there was a quiet moment while everyone drew breath before more guests arrived for the evening buffet.

The stars were blazing by the time they left their guests to enjoy the rest of the evening and take a quiet walk around the lake, Beau and Felix, for whom Paris was a move too far, snuffling in the long grass alongside them.

'Your first wedding, James. How was it?'

'Awesome. I'm so glad it was Fiona and Sean. Did we do well?'

'It's not too late for one or more of the guests to get falling-down drunk, or the bride and groom to have a hooley of a row, but all last-minute calamities were averted, the food was amazing and I think we can count that a success.'

'So you'll do it again?' he asked.

'In three weeks, if I've got the date right in the diary.'

'We're booked pretty solid through until the autumn. Is it too early to be thinking about something special for Christmas?'

'James, about Christmas—'

'I've been thinking about how we're going to decorate the place. And I thought we might have a carol concert for the village, mulled wine, food…'

'That's great. All lovely…'

James stopped. 'Sorry. You had something to say and I'm listening. Tell me what's bothering you about Christmas.'

'Not a thing, my love, but, before you get carried away on some wassail extravaganza involving paying guests, I think you should know that we're going to be having company.'

'Well, that's okay. We've got plenty of room. Who have you invited?' He paused. 'Your mother?'

'Not my mother. And you were the one who did the inviting.' He looked so confused that she finally took pity on him, took his hand and placed it on her waist. 'We're going to have a Christmas baby, James.'

For a moment he just looked at her, too stunned to speak. Then the words began to tumble out. 'Oh. Oh, good grief. That's incredible...' He put his arms around her and hugged her very gently, as if she were made of porcelain. 'I don't know what to say...'

'I know, my love. I know,' she said, putting her arms around his neck, her cheek against his so that their tears mingled and ran together. 'I am so happy I could weep.'

'That makes two of us.' He pulled back to look up at her. 'You've been holding that in all day?'

'It was Fiona and Sean's day, James. And I wanted us to have a little time to ourselves when I told you.'

'Good call. I'd have been an emotional basket case if I'd known.'

Chloe lifted her head as she caught the strains of 'Unchained Melody' drifting over the lake.

'I love this song. Will you dance with me, James?'

'I'll dance with both of you.'

He drew her close and, as she laid her head

against his shoulder, he began to hum the tune so that it vibrated through her body to the tiny being that was just beginning his or her life.

* * * * *

Look out for the next story in the
Christmas at the Harrington Park Hotel trilogy

Their Royal Baby Gift
by Kandy Shepherd

Coming soon!

If you enjoyed this story,
check out these other great reads from
Liz Fielding

Brooding Rebel to Baby Daddy
Crazy About Her Impossible Boss
A Week with the Best Man

All available now!